C000003038

This book is dedicated to my now deceased horse, Caribi.

February 24, 1993 – March 23, 2018

"You taught me the difficult art of dressage; we learned
together. You taught me to talk with horses, not just to them.
You taught me to live in the now. You and Mr. Monty Roberts
are the reason for the knowledge I needed to write this book!
You gave me the greatest experiences of my life within the
world of horses! You opened the world to me and gave my life
new substance. You are loved and admired by many, both in this
and in other countries! You brought me new close friends, like
family, across the Atlantic, and you made my life magical! You
were a once-in-a-lifetime horse!

Always in my heart, never forgotten!

Horses do talk - just listen and learn

A HORSE NAMED FLY

a story of learning a new language

A novel by Lena Vanessa

Copyright © 2023 Lena Vanessa

All rights reserved

The characters and events portrayed in this book are fictitious. Any similarity to real persons, living or dead, is coincidental and not intended by the author.

No part of this book may be reproduced, or stored in a retrieval system, or transmitted in any form or by any means, electronic, mechanical, photocopying, recording, or otherwise, without express written permission of the publisher.

Cover design by: The Fam. Noble-Antar and Lena Vanessa

Translated from Danish by Lisbeth Agerskov Christensen

Edited by Shaneen Noble-Antar

PREFACE

I have based this book on actual events. However, fictional elements have been added to emphasize the message of the book.

All names and places are fictional, and any resemblance to reality is coincidental.

It is my impression that in many places horses are trained using much more horse-friendly methods today than in the past. My desire for this book is for *even* more people to start to think of their horses as partners, although still as animals that are different from humans, who learn differently from us and who have a different "agenda" than we do.

Horses don't wake up every morning hot to trot for us to come saddle them, place a bit in their mouths, and ask them to work for us. But they can learn to like doing new things with us, learning new things, and discovering new places. Even so, it is our responsibility to teach it in a way that *they think* is fun.

Horses don't stand around the stall plotting to look mad when we bring the saddle, to toss us off into the water hazard on the show jumping course, or to buck as we break into a gallop. Horses don't think in abstract terms. They don't plan for the future. They are in the now. When they look grumpy at the sight of the saddle, it is because they remember that last time they wore it, it hurt. So maybe it's time to have the saddle checked by the saddler.

Horses live and act instinctively, and by understanding this and getting to know their instincts, we can develop a closer bond with our horses. For instance, in terms of survival it's important for horses to expend as little energy as possible on completing tasks. They must conserve energy in case they need to run away from a potential enemy that wants to eat them, or in case there is not enough food tomorrow.

The horse doesn't care who you are until you show that you respect him

CHAPTER 1
Will he go to slaughter?

Flying High had turned three years old. His lustrous chestnut coat shone beautifully in the sun. A bright white star lit up his forehead. He had a black forelock, mane, and tail, which he proudly waved and shook in the wind. His big, dark, almond-shaped eyes could shine with vitality, and it was clear to see that Fly was an intelligent horse.

Sadly, his eyes could also express deep fear, terror, and sorrow. That would happen when something reminded him of the horrible time at the racetrack where he had been treated with terrible brutality and hostility by the people around him. From time to time, he was downright abused. This horrible time had left deep scars on Fly's body and soul: he had become deadly afraid of people and of anything to do with people.

While Fly was still at the racetrack, it was determined that he was no good as a racehorse. The humans had agreed that it was impossible to break him, so he might as well be sold to slaughter. Of course, Fly knew nothing about this. And it was a good thing he didn't know, because he had experienced plenty of horror in his short life. He had been through an awful lot, and it was a wonder he hadn't lost his desire to live.

Fortunately, his life was saved in the nick of time by a young man whom nobody really noticed, but who would come around the racing stables from time to time. The young man made sure that Fly was sold to Alice and Jacob, just before he would have otherwise been sent to slaughter.

Flying High, the beautiful young thoroughbred, had lived for a few months with Alice and Jacob at the outskirts of a small idyllic town. It was a gorgeous sunny summer's day, when the horse trainer Sofia met Fly for the first time. Fly was enjoying himself with his beloved horse friends in the lush green pastures that bordered the forest. He was especially fond of one friend whose name was Sir Howard. Sir Howard was kind, helpful, playful, and full of tricks. He was solid as a rock, and good for hiding behind when necessary. Unfortunately for Fly, it was necessary far too often! Sofia picked up on this right away. She noticed that Fly expressed a terrible fear of sounds and movements that other horses found completely normal.

Sofia had many years of experience working with damaged horses. Horses whose lives had been bad for one reason or another. They were horses who had been abused, had experienced accidents that had scared them, had been misunderstood, or had just been poorly trained. She even managed to help horses that others had given up on.

Sofia had an innate ability to understand the animals. When she was with them, it was as though they understood her – as though she was speaking with them. She loved horses more than anything in the world. Thus, she had decided to work to give as many horses as possible good lives, and she wanted to work for as many people as possible who were learning to understand the horses better.

Alice and Jacob had made an appointment for Sofia to come out to evaluate Fly. They really weren't sure if he had been too damaged to develop a normal relationship with humans. After all, he had to be able to be handled if he was going to live a normal horse life.

So far, they hadn't managed to make significant

progress in that direction. Fly had dropped his halter in the pasture, and they couldn't get close enough to him to put it back on him. He was extremely skittish, and he always stayed on the opposite side of the string of horses. Not even feed, apples, carrots, or other treats could lure him over to them. After hearing Fly's story and getting to know him, they worried about how Sofia's evaluation would turn out. Could she help Fly, or was he too damaged from the racetrack?

CHAPTER 2

Flying High is Born

Fly was born on a beautiful spring day. The sun shone from a clear blue sky over the big pasture that was in a peaceful spot far from the outside world. It was an unusually lovely warm and calm day. The larks were flying around cheerily, warbling their song as they were building nests.

When Fly's mom, Sheila, felt contractions, she retreated a little from the other horses in the string. The other mares knew what was about to happen, and they let her be. They even made sure to keep their own foals from disturbing her. Even so, they kept an eye on her to make sure everything was going okay.

It was important for the survival of the entire string that everyone be ready to flee, should they be attacked by enemies. It was important that the birth be quick and easy. Fortunately, Fly was born without any problems at all.

He plopped down into the soft grass. The first thing he noticed was a warm, soft touch on his wet body. It was his mom licking him clean and dry. Fly thought it felt very nice, and he tentatively let out some tiny grunting sounds to express his pleasure. It didn't take many minutes, however, before his mom started to nudge him with her soft muzzle.

Fly didn't think that was too comfortable.

Hey, stop that! I am nice and comfortable lying here, he thought. But Sheila knew the potential danger if Fly didn't get on his feet in a hurry.

First, enemies could show up who might kill Fly. Secondly, it was important for a newborn foal to get fresh milk from its mother as soon as possible. The milk contained important nutrients, which the foal needed, both to protect it from harmful bacteria, but also to grow big and strong. So, she kept nudging him ... ever more insistently.

Okay, okay. I'll try, he thought.

Fly shook his pretty little head and got ready to stand. But it wasn't so easy to get up and stand on those long, thin legs that were folded up beneath him. Fly tried several times. First, one foreleg forward and push off ... bump, then he was flat on his side. Next, he tried to place both forelegs in front of him and push off ... bump, he fell again, and this time he rolled over, making all four of his legs stick straight into the air.

Noooo, I think I'll just stay right here, he thought, confounded. But before he could finish the thought, his mother nudged him again, and this time she even pushed him a little with one front hoof.

Fly made a tiny grunting sound and tried again. This time, he managed to get his long hind legs in under his body a little so he could push off with those as well. Voila! H e suddenly succeeded! Fly's legs were shaking and trembling, and they were far from each other. He felt himself starting to sway from side to side. He barely had time to think *oh, noooo,* before he was lying back in the grass.

He sighed deeply, but now he was getting stubborn, and he decided that *this time* he would succeed!

Once again, he managed to get both forelegs in front of him as he brought his hindlegs slightly up under his body. Then, he pushed off and suddenly he was standing. This time he was ready for the difficult task of keeping his balance. He kept his focus on that and on standing as still as possible. He almost held his breath as he slowly got himself settled on his long legs. After a moment, he was comfortable enough to move one foreleg … then the other foreleg, and that actually helped him balance better. Now he could move his hind legs as well. Even though he was very unstable (and it looked a little comical) he managed to take a few steps.

Whoa, this sure is tricky! Fly was using everything he had to avoid falling again. Getting up was so cumbersome that he really would rather not fall.

At the same time, something was telling him that it was critical for him to become good at standing and walking as quickly as possible. His basic instincts were letting him know. Fly managed to stay on his feet, and he was able to start moving all four legs a little. Soon, his instincts let him find his mother's udder. He realized that somewhere below his mom's belly was a source of food. He gently shoved his muzzle under Sheila's belly. The tiny nudges were signals to Sheila's udder that it needed to release milk. By using his sense of smell, Fly found the udder. He was wild with joy over finding food, and he was very hungry. He suckled away with all his might. His tiny black tail swung side to side with quick little movements of sheer happiness. Sheila made some loud sounds. Her udder hurt a little as the milk began to flow to Fly but it soon passed and after that, it felt quite nice.

The other mares realized that the entire critical foaling process had been perfect so far and life went on as usual, only with the little newborn Fly in the string.

The pasture was home to a total of fourteen thoroughbred mares and their newborn foals. The mares and their foals were put out to pasture every spring, where they would enjoy themselves all summer long, interrupted only when their owners checked on them occasionally. Sheila, however, had become pregnant so late the previous year that she hadn't foaled in time. As she was older and had foaled many times over the years without any problems, the owners were quite sure that she could foal in the pasture if they kept an eye on her regularly. Fly would be

Sheila's last foal as her owners had decided to retire her as a broodmare.

All day long, Fly scampered around, tumbling and playing on his unsteady colt legs along with all the other foals. They had a wonderful time in the green pasture. Fly thought his mom was the best in the whole world, and that he, himself, was the most wonderful colt to ever see the light of day. He was a confident little colt who had inherited his mom's leadership qualities.

Fly knew only his mother, the other horses in the string and of course, all the other animals that lived in and around the pasture. There were deer, rabbits, birds, and mice, as well as the funny, busy squirrels, the lazy cats, and the proud pair of bald eagles that would occasionally sweep in on their large wings. Everyone sought out the watering hole in the middle of the pasture to quench their thirst. The deer were agile. In their elegant way, they quite easily leapt over the fence around the pasture to drink and to enjoy the lush green grass. The horses enjoyed their days, and they didn't mind in the least that they were sharing their food and water with others.

Fly and the thirteen other foals developed nicely over the summer. They were growing fast, and they each developed their own personality. Even though they were eating more and more grass, they still enjoyed a little trip to the "milk bar" several times a day. In the wild, foals can be nursed by their mothers until they are a couple of years old, unless the mother has another foal. But Fly and his little friends were not living in the wild. They were owned by humans, and humans have plans for their horses.

CHAPTER 3
The Two-Legged Ones

On a cool fall day, some people arrived at the pasture in a big truck. Fly and the other foals had seen humans just a few times during the summer. They hadn't talked with their mothers about them; for Fly and the other foals, these humans were unknown creatures. Creatures that walked upright on two legs.

To Fly, it seemed like they had forelegs they swung as they walked. The "forelegs" didn't touch the ground and at the ends they had claws that could grab all kinds of things. They made unintelligible sounds with their mouths, and they had weird body language. They didn't act anything like any of the other animals that lived in the pasture. The grownup horses called them *"the two-legged ones."*

The two-legged ones came into the pasture and approached the horses together. Fly and the other foals were scared and hid behind their mothers. The mothers became uneasy. They knew full well that unpleasant things were underway. They tried to tell their foals what was about to happen: they were about to be separated, but there was no time to explain.

The two-legged ones obviously had a clear purpose for their visit.

Soon, Fly and the other foals realized that *they* were the purpose.

The two-legged ones seemed threatening and tried to

separate the string. They wanted to catch the foals and take them away from the pasture into the truck...to another pasture away from their mothers.

Ultimately, the mothers would be returned to the stables. Here, they would live until next spring until they would be returned to pasture after their next foaling.

Fly got scared. He tried to get away and hide. All the other foals did the same and there was chaos all over the pasture.

But the struggle was in vain.

Little by little, they caught one foal after the other, Fly included.

"Leave me alone, I want to be with my mom. I want my mom!" he screamed in his horse language. But the two-legged ones sounded as though they didn't hear him, or maybe they *couldn't* hear or understand him.

Fly struggled and struggled.

"What are you doing? What do you want from me? Mommy, help me!" Fly was yelling louder and louder.

Sheila was devastated that she couldn't help Fly, but she knew from prior years that there was no way around it. The two-legged ones outnumbered them and were far too strong for them to win the fight.

"You must be brave, my boy," Sheila yelled. "If you do as they ask, everything should be okay!" She was hoping to comfort him a little.

Sheila didn't know what would happen to Fly but she knew she would never see him again. She was afraid and despondent.

It was like this every fall. The foals were picked up and the mothers never saw them again. They were practically ripped from each other.

The two-legged ones did what they wanted, and they were the ones with the power.

If only they would give them a few days to be weaned, it wouldn't be such a big problem, and neither the mothers nor the foals would be so marked by it. When it happened in this violent way, it could damage the horses for life. Most of them were traumatized in a way that would affect them forever.

After the foals were loaded into the dark, narrow truck, it began to drive away. They were all so scared that they were at a complete loss as to what to do. The movements of the truck caused them to get tossed against each other. Struggling to s t a y on their feet, they knew they must do so if they wanted to survive in a world where they were prey among many hunters.

"Heeeelp!"

"Mooooom!"

"Ouch, you stepped on me!"

"Stop pushing!"

"Move over!"

The foals were yelling, all at the same time.

Despite the terrific noise from the fourteen foals in the truck, the sounds from outside were horribly frightening. They had no idea that these were just the sounds of other cars on the roads. Inside the darkness in the truck, it seemed incredibly scary and dangerous.

Aside from the noise caused by the wind as a result of the truck's speed, there was a loud whoosh whenever they passed oncoming cars, and the engine noise from the other cars echoed inside the truck – vroom, vroom, shuui, shuui … vroom, vroom.

Everyone was panicking and wanted nothing more than to get away – but it wasn't possible. It felt like they spent an eternity in this horror before they slowly started to tire and become quieter. Now they were focusing on just staying on their feet without bothering each other.

Fly noticed that the sounds from outside the truck had changed. "Listen," he said to the others. "There is not as much noise anymore!"

"You're right," one of them answered.

"It's much quieter," another answered.

"I wonder what's going on now," a third one said.

They had made it further into the countryside, where there was hardly any traffic. Suddenly, it seemed like the floor of the truck had disappeared beneath their hooves.

The truck had entered a gravel road with big holes in it. Even though it was driving slowly, the floor was bouncing terrifically every time one of the wheels hit a hole in the road. Of course, the foals had no way of knowing when it would happen, so they were tossed against each other; the ones that were on the outside were also tossed against the sides of the truck.

They were panicking again. "Ouch, ouch!"

"Oh no!"

"What is happening?"

"Heeelp!"

It felt as though the journey would never end.

CHAPTER 4

Life in the New Pasture

Suddenly, the truck stopped. It was completely quiet for a moment. But soon the foals heard sounds of the two-legged ones outside the truck.

The back end of the truck started to lower, and the autumn sun, which was low in the sky, poured into the dark box, blinding the foals with its sharp light.

The foals were frightened, and they were all trying to hide at the back of the truck, furthest from the opening.

They were all jammed together.

It didn't take long, however, before Fly realized that the door had opened to *freedom*.

He cautiously approached the opening, and his eyes grew wide with surprise! Freedom was out there! A big, open pasture, where the grass was still green! The sun was shining invitingly, and he headed down the ramp with a loud squeal.

"Wheeee, hurry! Come on!" he yelled happily to the others. The other foals were quick to follow Fly, and soon they were all racing along in a full gallop. Away. Away from the horrible truck and the two-legged ones.

Fly and the others were let out into a new pasture. A completely unknown place where they needed to get settled, yet they were so exhausted from the terrible experience that they needed to rest and gather strength first.

After a few hours, they started exploring their new

surroundings. They tried to find a way back to their mothers and their own pasture, but they found no possibility of getting away.

The pasture and the lovely little forest area they also had were bordered by a secure and strong fence. Exhausted and discouraged, they resigned themselves to their fate.

The next weeks were hard for all of them.

It was easier for some than for others but none of them got through the sudden separation and the transportation to the new pasture without scars.

It is unnatural for horses to be separated from their mothers or even their herds from one moment to the next. In the wild, foals are weaned from their mothers peacefully and quietly over a period. It can happen when she is getting ready to foal again, or when the foal is old enough to easily find its own food.

When the young horses are old enough, the young colts are slowly pushed out of the string. They live in bachelor bands until they're old enough to either form their own with mares or take over a group from an old stallion. The young mares are allowed to stay and be bred, or they are taken over by other stallions in new bands.

When humans separate horses from each other forever, to some extent, it creates lasting trauma for the horses. They experience it as a life-or-death situation. Their instincts tell them they must stay in the herd they know as that is where they know the hierarchy: who protects, who gets food and water, who educates, and – yes – who is in charge. Without the group, they don't feel safe, and it is very stressful for them.

Horses form friendships with each other, and they remember. They even recognize each other when they are reunited. They recognize each other's smells, sounds, movements, and appearance. Life would be *so* much more beautiful for horses if people were more thoughtful about this. There would be fewer horses with difficult dispositions; they would be far happier.

Horses should be weaned from their mothers slowly. They should learn that humans are part of the string, that they take care of them, provide water and food. Horses should be raised to live in the world of humans; to be together with humans.

By now, Fly and the thirteen other foals had been living in the new pasture and forest for eighteen months. They had a huge barn where they could find protection from the weather. However, they rarely used it. It was much more wonderful to be in nature. Plus, they had the forest, which provided the same comforts.

There was another reason the foals stayed away from the barn. It was a three-foot viper! Fly was the unlucky one who initially discovered the gray-brown viper. That day, the wind was strong, and it was raining cats and dogs. Even the leaves on the trees in the forest were bent against the rain, and therefore didn't provide much shelter. Fly went into the barn to seek shelter. He was just a few feet inside when he felt a terrible pain in one foreleg.

"Aaaaavyyy!" he screamed, bouncing backwards in fear. He just barely spotted the long grey-brown snake with the black zig-zag stripes down its back before he spun around on his strong hind legs and ran back out of the barn.

Fly ran as fast as he could out into the wind and the rain. He ran so far away that he figured the snake could no longer bite him. His strong flight instinct caused him to flee before he even had time to think about it. Better safe than dead!

When he stopped, he was gasping for breath. He lifted his head high, and he whinnied loudly to see and smell if the danger had passed, or if he needed to keep running. He stood there with the rain running down his dark fur, considering the situation.

All the other colts had run with him. Even though they had no idea what happened, they knew that when one member of the group took off like that, there was great danger close by and it's best to run. Later, you could investigate whether there actually *had* been any danger.

Hm, I don't think it followed me, he thought, as he kept sniffing, but there were no foreign smells.

"Yikes, I think I just cheated death!" Fly said to the others.

"What happened?"

"What was that?"

"Why did you run?" the others asked him fearfully, talking at once.

"I don't know, but something bit my leg. Ouch, it really hurts!"

Fly looked down at his foreleg, where the viper had bitten him. There were a few drops of blood in his hair, otherwise there was nothing to see. But it stung, and Fly could feel his leg starting to swell.

"Oh no, what's happening? I wonder if it is dangerous?" didn't know the answers to his own questions, and the others didn't either. He simply had to wait and see what happened.

After a couple of days, the swelling in his leg subsided, and it no longer hurt. Fortunately, nothing else happened, and Fly was back to being healthy and hardy. He would, however, remember the incident forever. It had taught him to be very aware of where he put his hooves, and he definitely wasn't about to go into the barn ever again. He would rather be chilly than risk being bitten.

Fly considered himself lucky that he rarely saw the strange, dangerous and mean two-legged ones which he had come to fear. The ones who spoke that unintelligible language and made weird movements with their bodies. Having a sharp memory, as horses have, the experience of the separation from his mother was still fresh in his mind. To Fly, the two-legged ones were predators; Fly and the other horses were prey. It was clearly safer to keep far away from them.

Soon it was Spring again and Fly turned two years old. Life in the pasture began to reawaken after a long, dark winter. The birds were singing and building their nests. The shy, silly long-eared hares were cleaning out their burrows in the bluff at the end of the pasture. The pheasant rooster was strutting around at the edge of the forest, looking to find himself a mate, and the frogs were croaking in the watering hole where all the animals quenched their thirst.

Once again, Fly and the others thought that life was wonderful. The colts frolicked and played, and, slowly but surely, they developed their natural instincts, becoming good at telling each other about their needs. They had established a hierarchy that created a safe and harmonious coexistence. They understood each other. They knew what it took to please, comfort, or anger others.

Occasionally, the hierarchy changed a little. That would happen when one of them felt ready to assume a higher position. Thus, they moved around a bit, but it didn't happen frequently, and the process was soon over, leaving everyone friends again. Although Fly was the youngest, his innate leadership instinct had made him the leader of the rag. He had a natural talent for creating a safe and harmonious atmosphere. He was good at being in charge, mediating between others when disagreements arose. He had a well-developed sense of justice, and he was great at making sure everyone was okay.

Then one day, *they* suddenly came back! Oh, no!

CHAPTER 5

The Trucks Return

Within a few moments, Fly's world turned into a living hell! The hunt was on. It was soon obvious to everyone that this time the two-legged ones were only looking to get Fly. With much fussing and fighting, five of the scary beings managed to separate Fly from the rag. All the horses were terrified.

The other horses crowde d together at one corner, watching with big, fearful eyes.

"Run, Fly, run!" they yelled to Fly.

And Fly ran.

He ran as fast as he could.

But they were tricky. They had brought ropes so they could surround him.

"What do you want? Tell me what you want from me," Fly tried to ask them once again.

But it was to no avail. They didn't answer.

"Leave me alone! I don't want to die!" he yelled loudly.

But it appeared that they were completely deaf! They didn't react the way Fly was familiar with in his world among the other animals.

When Fly had to stop to recover a bit from his complete exhaustion, they seized the opportunity and came down on him.

One of them had something in his weird claws that they wanted to place on Fly's head.

"NOOO!!!" Fly screamed, resuming his struggle to get away. He tossed back his proud head, raised his forelegs into the air, and kicked with his strong hind legs.

All for naught.

Fly lost his sense of direction, and he didn't know up from down. All he knew was that by now his strength was all but spent.

He had to give up.

They finally overpowered him and knocked him over. They put a halter on his head and attached a long string to it.

That's it, my life is over, Fly thought, barely able to see the other horses, who were still standing in their fear in the most distant corner of the pasture.

"Fly, Fly ..." they yelled.

Fly's distraught eyes were looking at them, but he didn't have the strength to answer them.

Fly was dragged, pushed, and pulled out of the pasture and over to the truck.

But he barely realized it.

The fear had released endorphins, which is a substance in the body that is somewhat sedating and calming. His body and brain were slightly sedated. He had become apathetic – without any way to work on escaping.

He vaguely noticed that he was brought into the truck. This time he wasn't let loose in there.

The two-legged ones had dividers that were pushed close against Fly's body. This was to help him keep his balance, while they were driving him. After all, this time he didn't have the other horses to support himself against.

Suddenly, Fly felt a tiny prick in his neck.

"Ouch!" he exclaimed startled, throwing back his head and causing his mane and forelock to billow through the air.

He didn't realize it, but he had been given a sedating shot. Not much, just enough to keep him calm during the transportation, so he wouldn't hurt himself if he panicked.

Fly felt very strange.

His thoughts were incoherent.

He could hardly feel his own body.

It seemed like sounds were coming from far away, and they were flowing together in a way he had never experienced before.

More than anything, he wanted to get away, but it was completely impossible. He was shut inside the truck, and it was moving.

Fly had no idea what would happen. He didn't know that he would never return to the pasture, or that he would never see his friends again.

In a moment, everything that was familiar was ripped away from him, and he was on his way to something completely unknown, where none of his friends were.

What would happen now?

CHAPTER 6
A Scary Future Awaits

Once the sedative loosened its grip and Fly came to, he was in a completely unknown world. The sounds, the smells, the light; everything was foreign to him.

More than anything, the tremendous, brutal, horrible *noise* was scaring Fly to death.

He was curled up in the corner of the little "box" he was in, which was a box in a stable.

WHAT is this? WHAT is happening? Where are the others? The questions flew through his anxious mind.

But there were no answers.

Now he noticed that there was something on his head. It was quite annoying.

He started shaking his head harder and harder, until his entire body was shaking along with it. It didn't do any good. Next, he tried to rub his head against his forelegs to get it off. But no matter how hard he tried, it didn't come off.

Fly didn't know that this was the halter that had been put on him when he had been overpowered in the pasture.

Suddenly, one of the two-legged ones showed up. Fly flinched and stared at it in fear. He was breathing quickly, ready to flee, but it stayed on the other side of "the box" and opened its mouth. Strange sounds were coming out of it, but the sounds were not like the ones Fly had heard before. The sounds were more pleasant this time – soft and round. This two-legged creature was smaller than the ones Fly had met in the past.

Fly was still guarded, but the sounds made him relax a bit, and he slowly managed to calm his breathing somewhat. He waited for it to talk to him in a language he understood. But it simply stood still, letting sounds come out of its mouth.

Well, Fly thought. *Let me try to talk to it.*

"What kind of creature are you?" Fly asked by sticking his muzzle out toward it but quickly drew back as it lifted a foreleg and stretched its claws toward him, which Fly took to mean "I am going to attack, skin, and eat you".

The two-legged creature pulled back the foreleg and stood there calm and still, watching Fly, before leaving again.

Whew, thought Fly, once it had left. *That was close. I think I'd better just be as quiet as possible and hide. But where can I hide? Where am I? This place I'm in is incredibly tiny. It isn't a pasture.*

Slowly, things quieted down. It was getting late in the day. Darkness was falling.

All the two-legged ones disappeared, and with them their strange sounds and horrific noise.

But compared to the pasture and the nighttime sounds of the pasture, this was a completely different kind of silence. A strange and scary silence.

Without him knowing, Fly had been driven to a racetrack. Just as Fly had no prior knowledge of the existence of these two-legged creatures and their trucks. Trucks that had brought him to strange places. Nor of the existence anywhere in the world of a noise as terrifying as the one he had just experienced; he also had no idea what a racetrack was. Good for Fly that he didn't know about that yet!

After a night in the strange silence, the sun came out. Slowly, Fly woke up from his slumber. He was awakened by a lovely sunbeam that reached him through a small window and warmed his shoulder.

Suddenly, Fly realized to his horror that he was still in the little "box."

Then it wasn't just a bad dream, Fly thought anxiously. How he missed the others from the pasture.

Right now, they have gone to the watering hole to drink, and soon they will go down to the eastern corner to start the daily walk through the meadow to fill their bellies with juicy grass, clover, and herbs.

The thoughts made him upset and sad.

Boy, I miss them! By the way, I am very thirsty and hungry. Where is the watering hole? Where is the grass?

Fly was starting to panic. He knew that without water and food he would not survive for long. Fly was abruptly torn from his thoughts when a horrible noise started.

He had never heard anything like it.

Help, what's happening? He thought, startled.

Fly was much too scared to ask anybody, and, as a matter of fact, he wasn't quite sure if there was anybody to ask who knew his language. He stood there, still as a pillar, with his heart pounding and his big, frightened eyes.

Soon, he heard loud crashes, knocking, and scraping against wood and iron. He heard harsh yelling by two-legged ones. Amid all this noise, Fly suddenly noticed a sound he recognized. He heard whinnying and whining.

"Hello!" Fly yelled.

His hope was renewed, and he yelled even louder:

"Hello, who are you? I am Fly. Come and help me. I have been imprisoned. Can you hear me? Help me!"

Fly whinnied and whinnied, but nobody came to his rescue. He was trying, through all the other racket to pick up what the other horses were yelling. But it made no sense. Why were they yelling: "Give me my food! No, I want mine first! If you come into my box, I'll make mincemeat out of you!"

What in the world are they talking about? Fly thought, continuing to wonder: *Why don't they just eat the grass? Because they obviously have grass.*

Suddenly, a foreleg from one of the two-legged ones

reached in over the edge of Fly's "box."

He jerked back into the corner, the only place he could find a little security. Just before the foreleg disappeared again, it left something in a little box on the wall.

Whoa, that was close. But what did it throw in there? He carefully stretched his neck and sniffed.

He didn't recognize the smell.

What you don't know can be dangerous. Fly knew *that* much.

When you are a horse and want to survive, you must be on guard and preferably flee from unknown things, until they have been proven safe. Period!

Little by little, things quieted down some. The two-legged ones disappeared again. In the silence, Fly could hear the sound of munching. Munching that he was sure came from the other horses eating. His hope was renewed.

"Can't anybody hear me?" he tried calling again.

To Fly's great excitement, a voice answered. The voice sounded sad, tired and a little rough.

"Yes, I can hear you, little one," it said.

"Where are you? Can't you help get me out of here?" Fly asked, excited and hopeful.

The voice told him that unfortunately it couldn't help, and by the way, nobody else could either. But Fly didn't give up just like that. Now, his hope had been renewed, and his fighting spirit was awakening in him. He wanted to know why nobody could help. He was used to at least one other horse always being ready to provide help.

The voice told him that his name was Winning Gold, Win among friends. Win asked Fly to eat the grain in the little "box", called a manger, and to drink water from the little iron thingamabob, the "water cup", which was situated next to the manger. All he had to do was push on it with his muzzle, then fresh water would come out.

"You go ahead and eat and drink, little one, then I will tell you where you have ended up."

Win gave Fly time to eat and drink when he realized that Fly must be both hungry and very thirsty.

"Thanks for your help, Winning Gold," Fly said, "Can I call you Win?"

"Sure," Win answered, "You are welcome to, but listen, and listen well, because this is serious."

In his wise and aged voice, Win began his long explanation about life as a racehorse on a racetrack, where horses were subservient to humans, the two-legged ones. It was a life where horses had to learn a bunch of new things that made no sense, most of which were completely opposite their instincts and nature. He explained that horses were only let out when it was time to work, and food was very different from what they were born to eat. Most importantly, there was no way to get help from each other.

Or at least that's the way it was in the stables *they* were in.

CHAPTER 7

Could it Really be True?

Fly listened with a sense of increasing horror. He hardly believed his own ears.

No...no, it can't be true. No life could be put on this earth, just to live like that. Who are they? Are they gods? Who can control other living beings without as much as asking us? We don't even speak the same language. How am I supposed to understand what they want? They are humans, after all, according to Win. It can't be true.

Win ended his sad explanation by assuring Fly that he'd better do his best to try to do what they want. He would need to forget everything he had learned thus far; in particular, he needed to try to curb his instincts. His instincts would cause him nothing but trouble.

"You are not going to meet a lot of humans who speak and understand your language. You should know that their language is extremely confusing, and they have a lot of different words that mean the same thing. It is difficult to understand the humans," he pointed out.

Even though he was just eight years of age, he was considered old, and, in fact, he felt very old and tired. Indeed, he had experienced and worked enough to fill just about twice that number of years.

Win knew that his time would soon be up. He knew that he would soon go for the last drive of his life. He had said goodbye to many of his friends over the years. Even friends who were younger than him when they were driven away, never to return.

Word around the stables was that the place where most racehorses were taken was a place where they lost their lives. Someone had heard the humans talk about a certain house when some of the others were driven away.

The humans called it a *slaughterhouse*.

In this slaughterhouse, the soul was released from the body; in this way all misery was over.

Win was discreet; he didn't tell Fly everything about the last drive.

"I am not doing it!" Fly thought, stomping against the concrete floor with one leg and throwing back his head, causing his forelock and mane to form a black cascade around him, his big black eyes shining in anger and determination.

"I'm not going to let them treat me that way. It can't be right. I'll show them. I will fight for my right to a dignified life, and for the rights of everyone else." Fly was a determined and strong-minded colt, but his sense of justice was about to take him through the most horrible experiences of his young life, and nearly to the slaughterhouse.

CHAPTER 8
What's the Big Deal?

Thoroughbred horses are bred to have a body and a mind to race. The humans believed that horses should be racing at just two years of age. Many humans also believed that Fly and horses like him would somehow know this automatically. If a horse didn't immediately understand what the humans wanted, they seemed to be confused. *So, what's the big deal?* They seemed to think. They assumed the horses automatically knew and agreed with their jobs. But for Fly there *was* a big problem.

Even though they looked as though they were fully grown, their bodies were not strong or developed enough to work with the same intensity as an adult horse. Also, they really needed more time to live a young, carefree life, allowing their minds to develop.

Fly was still just a kid, ready to become a teenager. It's hard for a child to be thrown into the adult world too soon, the way it happened to Fly.

CHAPTER 9
The Struggle Starts in Earnest

Like most horses, Fly knew a bunch of stuff as soon as he was born. He knew that he had to get to his feet quickly, so he could flee with the string in case of danger. He knew he could drink milk from his mother and where to find the milk. He also knew that he could show that he was little and defenseless by "flapping" his lips.

What he didn't know instinctually, Fly's mom taught him. She taught him the difference between what was dangerous and what wasn't. She taught him when to fight with his teeth and strong hind legs if needed or when he should simply flee. He learned that he is a prey animal. His mom also taught him about justice.

Fly hadn't learned anything from humans, as nobody had bothered to teach him. *No sense in wasting time on this,* the humans thought. *He will learn it when we need to use him.* They never asked if Fly wanted to learn.

Over the next couple of days, Fly gradually got used to the tremendous racket he could hear from the racetrack all day long. He got used to the food and the taste of the water from the weird water cup. Not that he liked it. He didn't like it *at all* – make no mistake about that. But there was no alternative.

However, he did *not* get used to the two-legged ones, who Win called humans. When they were in the stable, Fly felt very unsafe. He didn't know when they wanted something from him. When they were around his box, he retreated into the farthest corner.

Humans had given him nothing but bad experiences, and each time he had been in contact with them, horrible and sudden changes had happened in his life. Fly had prayed and prayed that someone would help him out of the box. But the day it finally happened, he wished he hadn't prayed so much.

A human came into the box. Fly flew into the furthest corner. He pressed himself up against the wall. But the human came closer, straight up to him, which Fly took in horse language to mean *I am unhappy with you, go away.*

Unfortunately, Fly *couldn't* go anywhere. *I can't flee, so I must fight,* Fly thought quickly. He threatened the human by taking a step forward and baring his teeth.

The human stopped briefly. *Oh, okay, perhaps it understands me after all?* But no, the human came closer.

Ok, he thought, *I'm gonna let you have it!*

He spun around and kicked at the human, striking one of it's legs!

The human wailed loudly and grabbed the leg, jumping up and down on the other leg. Since Fly had hit his target and the human was defenseless, all he wanted to do was flee. After all, he knew deep down that it was the only right thing to do.

Before Fly had time to do anything else, more humans came running, yelling and flailing their arms. They crowded into the box, and once again Fly had to jump into his "safe" corner. Here, he stood with his heart pounding and fear in his eyes, sensing that he was being treated unjustly. It made him angry and scared at once. The humans were also angry now.

They pulled back and made these weird sounds at each other with their mouths. Once again, their voices sounded angry and harsh.

"What do they want?" Fly yelled to Win, "I don't understand them. They are very angry!"

"They want to take you out of the box." Win explained.

"But they want to hold on to your halter. That's the thing buckled to your head. Fighting is no use, Fly! You must go with them, nice and calm. If you think they are angry now, just wait and see when they truly get mad..." His voice trailed off sadly.

Soon, another human came in. It was holding a long rope in its claws but Fly thought it looked like a snake. A very *long* snake, but a snake just the same. It had the same grayish-brown color as the snake in the barn at the pasture that had bit him on the leg.

Fly gasped loudly and held his breath. He couldn't flee, so he decided to stand there, perfectly still. *Then* it happened, the thing Fly had feared. The snake came flying through the air at breakneck speed *straight* at him. He ducked and jumped back, but the snake anticipated this, so it made a curve and managed to settle around Fly's neck. He jumped forward, tossing his head back and forth, up and down but the snake stayed put, and it got tighter and tighter. Fly fought as hard as he knew how. He spun around and around. He tossed his head around again and jumped back and forth.

Fly was starting to show the signs of the struggle. He was sweating, huffing, and whinnying. He was fighting the snake so hard that he completely forgot about all the humans in the box.

Suddenly, Fly was startled by a strong jerk from the snake. He lost his footing and flung his legs out in every direction but to no avail.

Bang! Fly was on the floor. Four humans threw themselves on top of him. One on his head. One on his neck. A third on his shoulder, and the last one threw himself over his hind quarters.

Fly panicked. As before, he was convinced that his life was over, and he wouldn't allow that! He summoned his last bit of strength and tried to get back up, but that was *totally* impossible with the humans lying on him like that. And they knew it.

After a bit of tumult, the pressure from the humans eased slightly. One of them made a short sound:

"Now!" And quickly, all four of them got up. Before they had time to blink, Fly was on his feet as well.

I survived, thought Fly, spooked.

"Win," he yelled with a shrill voice. "I survived. By the skin of my teeth, though."

"Take it easy, Fly. They aren't trying to kill you. They want to make money and..."

That's all Fly heard. He was startled by a very unpleasant and painful yanking over his nose and at his neck.

While he had been lying on the floor, the humans had attached a rope to the halter and around Fly's muzzle.

Their next goal was to get him out of the box. The biggest and strongest of the humans was pulling and yanking the rope fiercely, but Fly did what other horses do when they feel pulling at their neck: he pulled back. He pulled back with all his might, although it was tremendously painful for his neck and above his nose. He could barely breathe when the rope slid down and covered his nostrils. He fought and fought.

At times, he would almost sit down on his rear end when his hind legs would slip on the straw bedding. The pain was getting to be intolerable, but horses don't like to give in to this type of pulling. It is counterintuitive to them; Fly had not yet learned to temper his instincts as Win had advised him to do.

In his struggle, Fly failed to notice two of the humans sneaking up behind him. They were holding a rope between them.

Fly jumped forward when the rope hit his rear end. He felt like he was being attacked from behind by something unknown. The humans' trick resulted in Fly springing forward and landing in the aisleway.

Instantly, all the yanking, pulling, and attacks stopped.

Fly lifted his head so fast that his long black forelock billowed up in front of his face.

He looked around quickly, gaining an instantaneous overview of his new surroundings.

Hey, there *are all the other horses. Boy, there's a lot of them! Where is my new friend, Win?*

He soon had his answer.

He heard the familiar lifeless and rough voice.

"Hi, little guy. I am right over here."

Fly turned his head quickly, looking in the direction of Win's voice.

Fly eagerly started to move in his direction.

"Hi, Win. I am so glad to see you. I was about to lose my mi...."

That's as far as he got.

The big, strong human began to pull and yank at the rope again.

Fly was pulled around brutally.

His hooves slid on the concrete floor, while his head was pulled violently to one side. His legs were almost yanked out from under him.

The human didn't understand that he just wanted to see Win, so he could feel safer. Rather, the human was trying to show Fly that the human was in charge. It wanted Fly to behave and obey.

But poor Fly hadn't learned what they wanted him to do. Nor had he learned their sounds or language.

They are so unfair, Fly thought angrily. *Have they no courtesy in life? Can't they just ask me nicely for what they want me to do? Win is right. They* are *hard to figure out. What makes them think that they can boss me around? Why should I do what they want? Why can't* they *do what* I *want?*

There were no answers to Fly's many questions.

While this was happening, he suddenly noticed a large opening and the end of the stable. He could see grass on the other side of the opening.

Let me get over there! Then I can free myself and get away from this discomfort and confusion.

The colt took off at full speed and with renewed hope. His excitement at seeing the green grass surged, and he increased his speed. The big, strong human at the end of the rope was caught completely off guard. Now, it was the human's turn to lose his balance. *Smack!* The human hit the floor.

At the same time, one of the others yelled at the top of its lungs to some other ones that were standing at the opening at the other end of the stable.

Fly saw what was about to happen. He saw that the road to freedom was closing.

Now, he was angry. He lay his ears flat against his neck and sped his gallop even more, fighting for his freedom. But he was too late. The door closed just before he reached it. He was going so fast that he didn't have time to stop himself before crashing into the closed stable door. His hooves slid on the slick concrete floor, and he struggled to keep his balance.

Once he steadied himself, Fly stood shakily, covered in sweat, trying to catch his breath. In the meantime, more of the humans had come over to him. One grabbed onto the rope in his halter, while two others walked behind him.

They began to pull and push, and even though Fly fought back by shaking his head, refusing to move his legs, and trying to turn around, they managed with great difficulty to pull him down to the other end of the stable and into his box.

That was the beginning of Fly's introduction to life among humans.

The humans simply wanted Fly to stand tied up in the hallway of the stable to be curried and groomed. They wanted Fly to be fitted with a bridle, a saddle, and a rider. After all, millions of other horses had learned that before him.

To the humans it was no big deal.

In their opinion, this what was a thoroughbred horse was

born to do!

These humans had lived long lives with racehorses.

They sure knew how to "break a beast like Fly," in their words.

They *thought* they knew how to break Fly.

But they *didn't* know Fly.

CHAPTER 10

Not Everyone is Bad

Several weeks had passed yet Fly hadn't left the stable. He didn't allow them to curry him, and he didn't like the feed. He stood in his box, thin and dirty, downcast and sad. His eyes were dull, missing their sparkle and clarity.

His daily battles against the humans were hard on him. Even so, he fought them to a draw every time they wanted to get him out of the box, and every time they tried to put that nasty bridle on him. Win was the one who had told him that it was called a bridle and that he was supposed to wear it on his head. In fact, he fought them every time they wanted him to do anything, because so far, it had never been anything nice.

However, one of the humans was not like the rest. It was the human who had tried to talk to him the day after his arrival at the racetrack. It was much younger than the others and not so big and forceful. When it made sounds, they were soft and round. But Fly didn't understand the sounds. Nor did he understand the body language. He did sense, however, that this human was trying to communicate with him. And it had never done anything to hurt him.

When it came, it simply stood outside the box making sounds and looking at him with calm eyes. Sometimes it even came into his box. The first few times, it had scared Fly, and he had stood in the farthest corner with his head turned toward it. He was tense and ready to defend himself if necessary.

Although it never was.

The young human simply stood very still inside the door with its side facing Fly and its eyes to the floor. Occasionally, it collapsed completely, making it almost half its size. When it stood there like that, Fly would relax more and more. He sensed that it didn't want to hurt him, and that it was harmless like the animals at the pasture that shared their watering hole.

As the days went by, Fly discovered it was actually nice when the young human entered the box. He started to like these visits; the atmosphere in the box became calmer and more pleasant. He found himself relaxed enough to eat some of his hay during that time.

Some of those times, Fly had tiptoed carefully over to the human when it collapsed itself and was only half as big. He had stretched his neck out as far as he could. He had sniffed it and even touched it with his upper lip. The human had just sat very still, and Fly retreated calmly and started to eat his hay.

The fierce struggles with the other humans took most of Fly's strength. Because of this, he didn't have much energy to connect with the young human.

During the day the racetrack was chaotic and noisy. Humans were everywhere. Music blared through large speakers competing with traffic noise from the delivery trucks. Dogs barked and horses were constantly shuffled in and out of the stable.

When evening came, Fly watched the sun slowly disappear beyond the horizon through his small window and peace descended over the racetrack. It wasn't the stillness of his old pasture, but it was better than daytime.

Fly did find a bit of comfort in talking with Win and the other horses. When he stood close against the bars by the box door, he couldn't see Win, but he could see Fran the Fame, who stood on the other side of the aisle from Fly. He could also see Gilly Boy and Got to Run, who stood on either side of Fran.

Fran, Gilly Boy, Got to Run, and Win could all understand Fly's resistance to the way the humans handled him. But, as Win had explained to Fly the day after his arrival, there was no getting around it. They had no choice.

Horses must be submissive to humans; they had to accept the course of their lives. They had to learn to suppress their instincts and learn from other horses. None of them were very good at understanding human body language. Nor could they make sense of very many of the sounds from their mouths.

The other four horses had learned that if they couldn't or wouldn't obey a command, they were punished. Usually, the punishment involved pain. Humans made no threats before resorting to violent behavior like horses do. So, most of the time the punishment was completely unexpected, and they had no idea why they were being punished. They had simply tried to do what they figured the humans wanted. A lot of the time, they had to try to guess what the humans wanted from them. And if they weren't punished, they had guessed right. Then they just had to try to remember what the humans had done, so they could do the same thing next time.

No horses had come into the world to inflict pain on other creatures. Horses who did so learned because of the way humans had treated them. Horses and humans struggled to understand one another due to miscommunication, subjugation, or both.

Win, Fran the Fame, Gilly Boy, and Got to Run seemed older than their years. They had experienced too many horrible things in their young lives.

CHAPTER 11
Fran the Fame

Fran the Fame was the same age as Fly. She had arrived at the racetrack three months before he had. In that short time, she had been broken, she had submitted; she had lost her love of life.

She was born with a gentle, calm, and amenable disposition, and because of this the humans had moved quickly when doing things with her.

For humans, time was money, after all. The faster horses learned things, the faster the humans made money.

But strictly speaking, Fran hadn't *learned* things.

It had simply been done, and she had submitted, because it wasn't in her nature at all to fight against those who had the power. Fran only fought once: the first time a rider got on her back. She fought then!

Gilly Boy and Got to Run were just a year older than Fly, yet they had been through so much that they were very tired and felt all used up.

Fran the Fame, who was the latest one of them to experience what Fly was experiencing now and what he was about to experience, talked to Fly in her clear voice.

"The very day I arrived, they tied me up in the aisleway and put the bridle on me. I was terribly frightened, and I felt awful after the drive, but I couldn't explain it to the humans. I tried to show and tell them that I was scared, but either they didn't understand me… or didn't care to try." Fran paused briefly. She was getting a little sad, thinking about that day.

"The next day, they came back; they wanted to put a saddle on me." Her voice trembled at the thought of what had happened. "It was horrible, the first time they put that nasty saddle on my back. They didn't even tell me what they wanted to do. They just brought it and put it up there and tightened it hard around my belly. I was so scared and just wanted to get away, but I was tied up in the aisleway. When I jumped back, I got a fierce yank to the neck. My neck has been hurting ever since, and I don't know how to tell the humans in a way they can or want to understand," Fran let out a soft sigh and struggled to pull herself together.

"I have gotten used to the saddle," she continued, "When they first put it on my back, I thought it was a wildcat attacking me, but now I know that's not what it is. I just don't understand why the humans couldn't show it to me first. If they had taken more time and been kinder, it wouldn't have scared me so bad. Then I probably wouldn't have hurt my neck."

Gilly Boy, Got to Run, and Win expressed their sympathy for Fran. They felt bad that she was hurt and that the humans couldn't see that. They also felt bad that they had no way to warn Fran before it happened, but the humans had done things much faster with her than they had with the others.

"The saddle was a terrible experience, but it still wasn't as bad as the next thing that happened to me!"

Fly was angry for Fran.

These humans were heartless. Isn't there anyone on this earth who can teach them some decency? he thought. He almost didn't want to hear about any more of Fran's terrible experiences, but he couldn't help but listen to the rest of her story.

Fran told them about the fear of dying she felt the day she was brought outside and over to a tiny round sandtrack.

She had suddenly realized there was a creature sitting across her back. She hadn't even noticed the creature getting up there, it went that fast. She knew that wildcats attacked by jumping on your back so Fran assumed that it must be one of the dangerous wildcats.

Heeeelp! she screamed. *Heeeelp. I am getting eaten! I have been attacked!*

Fran did what horses do when they think they're being attacked by a wildcat: she took off at full speed, bucking. She bucked and bucked, spun around, and bucked again in her attempt to shake off the wildcat; but to no avail. The "wildcat" stayed put.

Slowly, Fran's strength waned, and she was terribly winded. She had to stop to catch her breath. When she had recovered a bit, she realized that it was a human sitting on her back, and not a wildcat at all. She was quite perplexed, because she had never heard of humans sitting on the backs of horses. She got scared once more, when it occurred to her that humans, like wildcats, are hunters, and therefore enemies.

As prey, you had to flee from hunters, be they cats, dogs, humans, snakes, or anything else. Therefore, Fran started again with her bucking and dodging.

"But the human was good and stuck. There was no way at all to buck it off. And the space was so small that I couldn't run very far. After a while I realized that I wasn't going to be eaten. Then I made peace with the situation.

Fran ended her story by agreeing with Win that humans are not easy to understand. She added that humans lack an understanding of horses.

Fly was shaken up and terribly sad for Fran the Fame.

Tomorrow, I must try to tell them about Fran's neck injury, Fly thought. *I can try with that human who makes the gentle, soft sounds.*

In his eagerness to help, Fly forgot his own problems for a bit. But the next day, Fly's own problems returned.

CHAPTER 12

The Plan to Break Fly

Every morning, there was a terrible racket in the stables. The sounds of horses kicking, stomping, and whinnying; humans shouting to each other, clanging feed scoops and buckets and the squeaking of wheelbarrows rolling across the concrete floor. Only when all the deafening sounds stopped and were replaced with horses munching on their breakfast, could Fly relax enough to eat as well.

Fly ate the pelleted feed the humans provided, though at first it hurt his stomach. He was used to pasture life, where he was constantly moving and foraging. Even though horses are large animals, they have delicate digestive systems. Bad feed, a change in feed or the wrong hay can kill a horse. Colic, either by obstruction or simply pains bad enough to send the horse into shock, can result in death.

Fly didn't know he had a slight case of colic. He just knew that his stomach hurt. When he felt the contractions in his stomach, he moaned, circled, pawed and rolled. Not only did his stomach hurt, but Fly was also distressed, exhausted and frustrated with the behavior of the humans, and their lack of understanding.

At the same time, the humans were planning their next attempt at getting him to cooperate. They could live with the fact that it was hard to get him out of the box, and that he was unwilling to let them brush him. They could even live with the fact that he was fidgety when standing in the stable isle, after all, he was mostly hurting himself when he pulled and yanked at the ropes that were secured to the walls on either side. But they couldn't really live with the fact that they couldn't get a bridle on him. After all, he wouldn't be able to race without wearing a bridle. The humans agreed to a plan that they were sure would break Fly.

"Ha-ha," one of them laughed as they walked down the hallway heading for Fly, "Now we've got him."

Fly saw them coming. Their expressions were focused, hard and threatening.

"Oh no, here we go again!" he yelled to Winning Gold and the others.

Fran, Win, Got to Run, and Gilly all lifted their heads with a start and looked out between the bars.

"Fly!" Gilly called, "Give up the fight! You can't win over them. It's not a great life we have, but at least we're alive. Maybe one day we'll be lucky enough to be free, so we can find a herd to live with. Free, so we can get the mares foaling, so we can make sure there will always be horses. But to do that, we need to survive. Give up the fight, Fly! Don't risk a trip to the slaughterhouse."

Slaughterhouse? That made no sense to Fly. He understood the other things just fine. Afterall, freedom was his goal; it's why he fought so hard. *Give up the fight?* No, he wouldn't do that. If the humans didn't treat him properly and decently, they shouldn't expect him to behave properly and decently.

It may have been different if they had handled things differently. If only they had introduced themselves to Fly in a way that was familiar to him. Perhaps they could have put some effort into understanding his language.

The key to communicating with horses is body language. As a human, it's all about the way you stand, where you rest your gaze and the way you approach them. For horses, it's simply about the way you move your body, your legs, your ears, your eyes, your head, and your tail.

How hard can it be? thought Fly.

Now, the focused humans were just outside Fly's box. Their eyes were turned straight at Fly. They were twisting their lips in smiles that looked menacing. To Fly, it looked like they were baring their teeth. When they did that while standing square in front of him, what they were saying in horse language was: "I'm warning you, I will attack you if you don't get out of here."

By now, Fly was learning to ignore this "phrase" from them. They often stood like that. He was aware that they had *no* idea what it meant. In fact, they didn't react when Fly, himself, stood that way in front of them.

The humans had come up with a plan to break Fly. They believed they needed to break him before they could put the bridle on him. They hadn't considered at all if there were alternative methods. As mentioned, they had been working with thoroughbreds for many years, and they did what they usually did. It usually worked out one way or another very quickly.

They hadn't given it one thought that the horses could and would perform better if they learned to enjoy doing the work, rather than being forced. They hadn't considered teaching the horses to *want* to do the work. These humans saw the horses as a source of income and prestige. They treated horses as if they were stupid and had no feelings.

By now, Fly knew what was going to happen when they got into the box with him.

I get so scared every time the throw that snake over my head, he thought. He tried to give himself more courage.

But on the other hand, I am not about to go with them voluntarily. Why would I do that? There is always something unpleasant waiting for me.

So, he fought against the snake like he always did.

As usual, he surrendered when he realized that the fight

was hopeless. The moment he quieted he felt a prick to the neck.

"Oh, ouch!" he yelled, throwing his head high into the air. *What in the world are you doing to me now?*

The humans laughed in a mocking tone. They had given Fly an injection with a bit of sedative that worked after a few seconds. Fly became dizzy and sweaty, his legs felt like jelly. His thoughts slowed down and sort of drifted away before he had time to catch them. He wanted to ask Win what was happening to him. What they had done to him. But somehow, he couldn't get out the words. He couldn't form the thoughts.

Fly had a foggy notion that he was being brought out of the box. There were humans everywhere around him. They were pushing, pulling, and yelling at him. He was so hazy, dizzy, and unstable on his feet that there was no way for him to resist.

Somewhere deep inside, he knew that this was not good. He knew that when he was weakened, which he was from the sedative, he was unable to follow his instinct to flee when he was in danger.

Even though Win says they aren't going to kill me, it sure feels like it! Fly thought in his foggy mind.

Out in the aisleway, Fly felt something cold and heavy placed in his mouth; something was pulled over his ears. Not long after that, he was coming to; the sedative was wearing off.

"Now, what is this? Oh no, what did they do? What is going on?" Fly yelled, scared.

Usually, experiences happening while being sedated are frightening to horses, since they have had no way of following the course of events, and their ability to flee is taken from them. This was exactly how Fly experienced the bridle.

Win had witnessed everything. Even though he admired Fly for his fighting spirit and strong will, he still shook his head.

"Fly, I am sorry, but as we told you, fighting against them is futile. They have put a bridle on you. You need to have that on your head when they ride you," he explained.

"Ride me? What do you mean?" Fly looked at him scared. Win explained it to Fly.

"Remember what Fran told us? They sit across your back, and then you are supposed to run with them."

"Run with them? Why would I run with them on my back?" Fly was completely confused now, and he didn't understand what Win was talking about.

"You are supposed to race other horses," Win answered. "The humans want for the horse they are riding to be first to arrive at the place they call the finish line. They must put the bridle on you, so they can steer you to that place."

Win wished with all his heart that he could help Fly, but obviously he couldn't.

Now, Fly saw one of the humans reach for his head and ears with its claws. He did what he always did when they made that movement. He threw himself to the side, jumped forward, and threw his head hard backwards. He did *not* like it when they attacked him that way.

The humans lost their patience once again. Two of them held each side of his bridle and pulled down as hard as they could. One of them got a good grip on Fly's one ear, which was squeezed and twisted hard.

"Ouch, ouch!" Fly yelled, shaking his head to get free. "Ouch, let go of me!"

But the human held on tight.

When the struggle ended, Fly discovered that he was no longer wearing the bridle. Now, the only thing left was the halter he had been wearing the whole time. He shook his head, making his forelock billow. He shook so hard that he could feel it in his entire body. All the way down to the back hooves.

Oh boy, that was a horrible experience. I am not letting them do that again, and I don't want them to pull my ears!

Fly didn't finish his thought before the humans tried to get the bridle on him again. He fought again, like he had done earlier. The humans were trying to hold his head down. Everyone was huffing, groaning, and sweating. It was all very violent.

Suddenly, Fly felt a burning pain on his thigh. It startled him, and he jumped forward as far as the rope he was tied with allowed. The humans holding his head were knocked over and started to yell.

Smack.

The pain returned.

Smack, and again, and again.

Fly, who was completely confused over this unexpected attack, threw himself around in the rope.

Smack, smack, smack. The attack continued.

The pain was horrible, but the fact that Fly was tied up and couldn't flee was even worse.

As a prey animal, Fly knew that he absolutely had to get away! Afterwards, he could stop and figure out what was causing the pain.

Smack, smack.

Fly couldn't associate this type of attack with any predatory animal he knew. This made it even more difficult to decide what he should do.

He didn't know that the humans were hitting him because they were angry that he wouldn't stand still and because he didn't want them to put on the bridle.

Smack, smack, smack. The strikes from the whip continued. When fleeing was impossible, defending himself was his next reaction. Flight or fight. Because of this, Fly now kicked back with one hind leg. He couldn't see what he was kicking at, and he didn't hit anything on his first try. He tried again immediately, and one more time just be sure.

No horses are born with the inclination or thought to harm anybody or anything. But if they are forced to do so, their reaction is lightning fast, and humans are way too slow to get to safety. He knew he had hit something when he heard a wail from one of the humans. The sharp jolts of pain on his hind quarters stopped as suddenly as it started. But now, two other humans jumped on him from the front. They were yelling and screaming.

"You devil! *That's* enough!" They punched Fly's head and neck with their claws in a fist.

Fly jumped back while tossing back his head as far as the rope would reach. He felt a bad crack in his neck, but he didn't register the pain. He was far too focused on evading the attack.

But there was no way.

The humans were very angry and wanted nothing more than to "put Fly in his place". One jumped forward once again managed to get a tight grip on one of Fly's ears. The anger of the humans seemed to give them more strength, and Fly's struggle to free himself lasted longer this time. But with huge effort he succeeded.

The fight stopped suddenly!

Now what? thought Fly. *Where will the next attack come from?*

He stood there, huffing and with large, fearful eyes, looking around, tight as a bow. Sweating, out of breath, and shaking all over his body, he was anticipating a new attack.

Smack!

There it was again, the burning pain on his thigh.

Fly flinched. Along the way, he realized that the burning pain came from one of the humans, who was using a whip on his hind quarters.

Suddenly, it was over. The humans stood, lay, and sat all around Fly, panting and moaning in pain and exhaustion.

The young human who was friendlier than the others had been standing at a short distance and watched in fear and sadness. Very quietly and scowling at the humans, he now approached Fly.

Fly stood there out of breath, watching him get closer.

It probably isn't dangerous. It has a different expression than the others. And it has never done anything to hurt me.

The young one reached up very carefully and loosened Fly from the rope. He held the halter gently and turned around slowly, thereby inviting Fly to follow, which he did.

Once back in his box, Fly was completely exhausted as he stood there sweating, out of breath, and scared. *Why are they like that? Why?* he thought again and again.

Fly's strong survival instinct and sense of justice were now the reason why the humans made a fateful decision. A decision that would change Fly's life forever.

CHAPTER 13
The Slaughterhouse

The humans agreed that Fly was stupid, stubborn and dangerous; unable to learn anything at all.

"By now, we have fought with him every day for months on end, and he still doesn't understand anything. That wild, stupid beast is only fit for the slaughterhouse. He will never be a racehorse! I bet he can't even run fast enough!"

They made arrangements for Fly's transport to slaughter for the very next day.

"Ha, that stupid beast … he will get what he deserves!" said one of the ones Fly had kicked.

The young human who had tried to befriend Fly heard what they were saying. It made him angry, but also devastated for Fly.

I must do something! Fly is nothing like they say. It's just that they don't understand that he is very smart and that he is simply following the instincts deep down inside him. Oh, if only they would listen a little and learn from others. Fly will not *be slaughtered!*

After a couple of phone calls, the young human was reassured. He had talked his foster parents into looking at Fly and perhaps buying him from the horrible owners who just wanted to slaughter him.

I hope Alice and Jacob will buy him! He will have a good life with them. At least they understand horses, and they *seek help and advice if they run into problems they can't solve. Fly deserves to be understood.*

That night it was dark and cloudy. The rain fell steadily and quietly, going *pling, pling, pling, pling* all night long on the metal roof. When the wind blew around the raindrops, it sounded like a little tune – *pling-pling, pling, pling-pling, pling, pling.*

Fly slept fitfully and had nightmares. His dreams reflected all the ugly experiences he had been through. He woke up several times, only to look around in fear before falling asleep again after making sure that he was still alone in his box. But the nightmare started again every time he fell asleep.

The nightmare was always about him being chased by something unknown. He tried to run from it, but it was as though he couldn't run very fast - like he hardly moved. The scary dangerous and unknown pursuer kept getting closer and closer, but it was invisible the whole time. Sometimes the nightmare ended with him falling into a big hole. He kept falling and falling and falling, before waking up with a big start. He always felt miserable after one of his nightmares.

Fly heard the faint sound of Got to Run calling from the other side of the hallway.

"Fly ... Fly, are you awake?" Fly slowly woke up. He felt sore, beat up, and very sad. The experience of the prior day was still fresh in his mind, and all his muscles were aching after the long, violent struggle. The skin on his hind quarters where the whip had attacked him over and over was swollen and very, very tender. In fact, standing on his left hind leg hurt, so he just didn't. His neck was terribly sore as well. The pain gave him a headache that shot down his neck and out into his back. Fly's top two cervical vertebrae been displaced when he fought against the ropes the day before. His mouth and throat were completely parched, and his tongue felt swollen and rough.

Carefully, slowly, and very painfully he moved over to the water cup on the wall. After he quenched his thirst and felt a little better, he had enough strength to answer Got to Run.

"Hi, Got to Run. Yes, now that you woke me up, I'm awake," Fly said dryly.

"Ha-ha," Got to Run laughed, "I can tell that you haven't lost your sense of humor, ha-ha. I just want to say that I think you're the bravest little horse I ever met! You sure do have courage and heart. Even though I am afraid it will be your undoing, I hope with all my heart that it brings you happiness instead. If anyone deserves it, you do!"

I feel so bad for Got to Run. He must put up with so much injustice, simply because he is fundamentally created to please! Fly thought, but he didn't say it.

"Thank you, sweet Got to Run," he said kindly, fighting the fatigue in his voice. "It's good to hear something nice instead of all the things I'm not so good at. After all, I already know about those. If everyone were as nice as you are, the world would be a much better place. It is also my opinion that we might as well treat each other with decency, dignity, and respect. After all, we are all born equal. Nobody is born with the right to control the life and fate of another. Got to Run, promise me one thing. Always make sure you have friends to have a good time with! Will you promise me that?"

Got to Run didn't answer right away. He needed a moment to understand what Fly had said.

"You're right!" he said, "I never thought about it that way. I always thought that the strongest ones made the rules. We all have a right to a good life. If anything, I suppose the strong ones should be protecting and guiding the not so strong ones".

Got to Run stood for a long time, pondering the relationship between humans and horses.

After breakfast, Fly slowly regained his strength. He was still sore all over his body, however, and that would continue for a few more days. He hoped with everything in him that the humans would leave him alone today. Even though he protested so fiercely against the humans' treatment of him, he had become very afraid of them. Who wouldn't fear those who constantly subjugated by inflicting pain and bad experiences? Who wouldn't fear those who at every encounter appeared ruthless?

Fly didn't realize that the humans had already decided what would happen to him; his fate was sealed.

As on any other day, this day was filled with continuous noise as one hears at a racetrack. Because of this, Fly didn't notice the sound of the horse transport, when it arrived around noon. This transport truck had arrived to haul Fly to the slaughterhouse. It was the truck the humans had ordered the day prior.

The young human had asked Fly's owners to wait before sending him off. He explained to them that some people would come who might want to buy Fly. The impatient owners didn't really want to wait. They didn't believe that anybody would buy a stupid and useless horse like Fly. The young human explained frantically that they could get more money for Fly than meat prices, even though he wasn't quite sure about it.

More money! Now, that was something that tickled the ears of the owners! They agreed to wait for one hour.

Whew! I hope Alice and Jacob will be here soon, the young human thought.

He didn't have to wait long, because at that moment a tall, slim, dark-haired lady stepped in through the wide door at the end of the stable. She was accompanied by an even taller man with broad shoulders. They both exuded peace and harmony. It was Alice and Jacob.

CHAPTER 14

Fly's New Humans

Alice and Jacob lived in a small town not too far from the racetrack. On their farm, they had a mixed string of wonderful horses. There were horses of every size and of different breeds. In addition, there was their dog Benji, four cats, and several chickens. Finally, there was their kind foster son, Nicholas.

Nicholas frequented the racetrack off and on because he liked to visit the horses. As luck would have it, he was there during the time Fly was there. Fly knew him as "the young human." Nicholas had been the one who saved him.

Alice and Jacob had a good understanding of animals and were skilled in communicating with them. They had a deep love for animals and believed that the strong should protect the not so strong. They couldn't bear the thought of Fly being slaughtered. They could see immediately that this was a little horse who was scared and misunderstood, but who was otherwise healthy and hearty.

Soon, they were standing outside Fly's box. "What's the price?" Alice asked. Though the owners quoted an unreasonably high price, Alice and Jacob didn't want to negotiate. They simply paid the money to the greedy owners.

Now, Fly belonged to them. But how would they get him back to the farm? Nico told Alice and Jacob that there was a truck outside that had been ordered to take Fly to the slaughterhouse. He suggested that they could ask the driver to take Fly back to their farm.

"That's a great idea, Nico," Jacob said. "Let's ask him."

They made a deal with the driver. Next, they had to get Fly into the truck.

"Hmmm, we need to think about this," Alice said, "Nico, you know Fly best, how do you think we can get him on the truck?"

Nicholas told her Fly was a smart and inquisitive horse, and that he was sure that if they backed the truck all the way up to the end of the stable by the large door and gave him plenty of time to understand what they wanted him to do, he would load up. But he also warned them not to pressure Fly too much. He had seen how Fly's eyes had turned black as coal and hard when he was pressured, always leading to an attack.

"I think I can get Fly to come with me," Nicholas said, "at least I would like to try."

The others thought it sounded like a good idea, and the truck was backed up to the door. Alice, Jacob, and the driver stayed just outside the stable so Fly couldn't see them. The former owners shook their heads and left.

Nicholas went into Fly's box and squatted with his side facing him.

"Fly ..." he called in his gentle voice, "I know you don't understand what I'm saying, but I want you to know that we are helping you. You will be driven away from here to a home with us where you will have a good life with other sweet horses. I will do whatever I can for you every day, so you will be happy."

Fly was still sore all over after his struggles with the other humans the day before, but he wasn't scared when the young human came in to see him. He listened and relaxed, becoming inquisitive, he stepped closer. He stretched his neck toward the small human, sniffing him, making little chewing motions and licking his lips.

Nicholas sensed and heard the motions more than he saw them, because he kept looking at the floor to avoid scaring Fly. A stream of happiness surged through him, and tears of joy welled up into his eyes.

When horses make chewing and licking motions, it often means that they are letting go of tension and relaxing. It's a sign of happiness.

What Fly was saying in horse language was: *It's nice that you are here. It calms me down, and I don't think anything bad will happen as long as you are here with me!*

After sitting for a while, Nicholas had a hunch, almost like somebody had whispered to him. *If you get up slowly and leave the box calmly, Fly will come with you.*

For a moment before Nicholas got up, he tensed up a little. It would be a miracle if Fly would go with him, and maybe even go all the way into the truck. Quickly, he pushed the thought away and focused fully on keeping his breathing calm and slow and moving slowly, but without hesitation.

Well, here we go again! Fly thought. But then he saw that something was different. This time, the door to the box wasn't closed. The human walked a distance away and then stopped. It stood calmly with its side facing Fly and its eyes to the floor. It held its forelegs in front of it with its claws tucked under.

Now, what is this? Fly lifted his beautiful head and looked from side to side while sniffing with his big nostrils, but he could neither see nor smell any kind of danger. There were only the young human and the other horses.

He walked toward the open door, stuck his head out the door, and looked around. He was on alert! What if some of the other humans suddenly showed up, or if the snake came flying to capture him again?

Fly looked over at Fran, Gilly, and Got to Run, who were standing across from Fly's box. They were keeping an eye on what was happening.

"What do you think is happening?" Fly asked them.

Got to Run was bemused.

"I really don't know. I have never experienced the humans opening the door and just walking away!"

Fran and Gilly had no explanation as to what was happening either.

Fly left the box, hesitantly and slowly. He was tense and guarded. It was scary when something new and very different suddenly happened. He had no idea what to expect.

The young human made a gentle sound, reached out toward Fly with one foreleg, pulled it back again and turned around slowly, walking down the hallway of the stable, away from Fly.

To Fly, it seemed a little like when he and the other horses in the pasture invited each other to come along. He thought about it for a minute and decided to walk down the aisleway. He was still on alert, however, and he looked around nervously.

Calm and without hesitation, Nicholas continued down to the end of the stable, up the ramp, and into the well-lit truck; it looked bright and friendly. Here, he stood with his side facing Fly and in a relaxed posture, like he had done outside the box.

When Fly reached the truck ramp, he hesitated for a moment while he considered what to do.

I have never experienced being hurt by the young human and anything must be better than staying here! I'm going to go with him.

Everyone breathed a sigh of relief as Fly entered the truck and the ramp was closed.

CHAPTER 15

Fly's New Home

Back on the farm, Fly was let into a large pasture filled with lush green grass. Alice and Jacob's other horses stood watching from the adjacent pasture.

The pastures were in a peaceful location behind the white-washed barn, which, after the harvest, would be full, floor to rafters with green hay and soft straw. There was a watering hole between the two pastures with water that was always fresh and cool, just as Fly remembered as a baby at pasture.

The forest, which bordered three sides of the fields, was in full bloom, and there was lots of activity from deer, foxes, squirrels, all kinds of birds and hares. As Fly had known from growing up in a pasture, the other animals came to the watering hole to quench their thirst. The frogs croaked as the sun slowly set.

However, Fly paid no attention to all of this. Even though he had entered the truck voluntarily, the drive had been frightening and unpleasant. He didn't see the lovely grass that he had been longing for so much during his time at the racetrack, because he was much too scared to eat. He feared the worst. He had no reason to do anything else. Until now, every change in his life had been for the worse.

As he gazed around his new surroundings, Fly suddenly noticed the horses on the other side of the fence. He trotted over to them excitedly, calling to them.

"Hi!" he said, "I'm Fly, who are you?"

There were four other horses in the pasture. There was Lisa, a beautiful fjord horse. She was the modern type with the familiar yellow color and the narrow black stripe running from her ears down through her mane, and all the way to the tip of her tail. Scamp stood by her side, Lisa's two-week-old colt. He looked like his mom in every way. It was obvious, however, that he had inherited his father's eyes.

Scamp's father, who was now a gelding, was there too. He was a big, handsome, and muscular Knabstrupper named Sir Howard. He was brown with a few, distinct white spots on his hind quarters. Around the big, gentle, almond-shaped eyes his skin was soft and pink.

The fourth horse was a Danish warmblood mare, Alexandra. She had a noble, finely formed head and wise eyes. On her forehead was a pretty little star, and there was a precious little patch on her muzzle. Alexandra was expecting her first foal within three weeks, so she was a little heavy and encumbered. Despite her pregnancy, Alexandra had maintained her position as leading mare in the string. This was due to her being the oldest, and she was still healthy and hearty.

Being the leader and the highest in the hierarchy of a group of horses entails several things. In fact, it isn't an enviable status, even though it gives the right to eat, drink, and choose a place to sleep before the others. Because it also entails responsibility. Responsibility for the survival of the herd. Responsibility for the well-being of all. Responsibility for the good behavior of everyone. Responsibility for protection of the weakest. Alexandra was successful in maintaining all of this in her string.

Despite thousands of years of life and breeding in captivity, horses still live according to ancient instincts. These instincts survived from the time when horses lived freely and without human interference in the wild. They were born out of life in nature, often harsh alongside their natural enemies, the predators. Food and water could be scarce, and there was nobody but themselves to make sure they survived and reproduced.

Every horse still lives according to the ancient flight, food, and herd instincts. In other words, even today the life of a horse is about two things – survival and reproduction.

CHAPTER 16

Fly's New Friends

All four of them flocked together at the fence into Fly's pasture, but Alexandra stood closest as she was the leader. She used her posture to keep the others back a little and outside of any danger. She didn't know Fly, and she didn't know if he was friend or foe. She let out a deep, long, and calm neigh. After just a few seconds, however, she sensed that this was a young and frightened little horse.

"Welcome, my little friend," Alexandra said with her calm and gentle voice. "Don't be afraid. I am Alexandra and I am the oldest of us. Where are you from?"

Fly was still afraid and shaken up. The adrenaline was pumping around his body, and he could barely register anything else. He could tell immediately, however, that Alexandra was the leader. He kept a deferential distance to her and avoided eye contact as is required to show respect.

"I am coming straight from the racetrack. Ugh, I don't hope to be going back there. It is a terrible place. Have you ever been there?" he asked, his voice shaking.

"I have been to lots of places, but never to a racetrack," Alexandra answered. "But take it easy, little Fly. For now, you are safe; we are happy here." She turned her body, so her side was facing Fly and lowered her eyes. She was showing Fly that he was welcome in her little band.

Fly let out a deep sigh, made chewing motions with his mouth and lowered his head. This way, he was showing

Alexandra that he had understood her, and he already knew that with her things were safe and nice.

I'm so glad to escape life in that tiny box. I sure missed having contact with other horses. It's very lonely when there is nobody else to talk to, groom and play with! Fly thought, as he stood there showing Alexandra deference.

Lisa, Scamp, and Sir Howard stood in the background, witnessing everything with curiosity. Sir Howard realized that Alexandra had accepted Fly, and he also knew that Fly had accepted the offer to come under her protective wings. Now, as the second-highest horse in the hierarchy, he could step forward to greet Fly. Sir Howard bid Fly welcome in his deep, pleasant voice.

"Welcome Fly, you poor fellow. You're terribly thin and dirty. We'll get you back into shape. Don't doubt that for a minute," he said kindly.

Sir Howard turned his head and pointed to his round, full belly with his muzzle. "As you can tell by looking at me, there is plenty of food here!" he laughed.

Sir Howard then stood up on his strong hind legs, spun around, and took off at full tilt, squealing and laughing. As the jokester and teaser, he was, he wanted to lighten the atmosphere a little.

"Heee-heee-heee. Life is wonderful and the grass is green. Heee-heee-heee." Everyone else laughed, both horses and humans. The slightly repressive mood lifted.

"Oh, that Howie!" as they called Sir Howard. "He is always full of fun and in good spirits. You can count on him," Jacob said.

"Yeah," Alice said. "You can count on Howie. He's got it all. He is also good at interpreting situations. But I hope he didn't scare Fly."

Alice, Jacob, and Nicholas looked at Fly. But Fly had also sensed the mood lightening, and he began to relax. It would take a long time, however, a very long time, before he felt safe.

Unfortunately, it was impossible for him ever to feel *completely* safe. The horrible experiences he had been through stayed with him for the rest of his life. The experiences could be relegated to the back of his mind, but they would always be there, occasionally resurfacing.

Fly had a good memory; it helped him survive. He could remember both good and bad things he experienced.

Lisa and her foal, Scamp, had followed everything from a distance. Scamp was just two weeks old, so Lisa protected him from any dangers, but like all the others, Lisa sensed that the situation was calming down.

She gave Scamp a gentle nudge with her muzzle.

"Scamp, honey. We can relax now. Everything is under control. That new guy, Fly, is nice, but remember, little Scamp, he is older than you. That means that he knows more about life than you do; he will look after you, protect and warn you when danger is afoot. That's why you must respect him," she said.

Scamp lifted his head high into the air, raised his short foal tail straight up into the air, and bounced around his mother.

"Okay, mom. It sure is nice to have another horse to look after me. Do you think he will play tag, mom? Do you think he will?" he asked eagerly with his clear little voice. Lisa laughed.

"He might want to play tag with you, honey, but remember to ask nicely. When you do that, you get a nice answer back," she said.

Once Alice and Jacob were sure that everyone was relaxed, they decided that Fly should be allowed into the enclosure with the other horses. When the gate was opened, Alexandra went into the pasture to Fly. Next, Sir Howard and Lisa followed, and finally Scamp came through the gate. Fly retreated slightly as Alexandra approached him. Alexandra stopped, looked at Fly, and decided that there was no danger in allowing him to join the string. She placed herself sideways to Fly and avoided looking at him. This told

Fly that he was welcome to approach Alexandra, and that he was allowed to become part of the string.

Fly lowered his head. That way he was showing that he was accepting Alexandra's invitation, and he showed that he accepted her as his leader by making chewing motions. After this, he walked over to her, slowly and calmly. They sniffed each other, and once again Fly made chewing motions. Alexandra rubbed Fly's mane with her front teeth to welcome him.

"Welcome!" Alexandra said. "As long as you adjust to the string, we are happy to have you here. The more of us, the better we can look after each other and stand guard when we eat and sleep."

Sir Howard had watched in silence. Now he reached out to Fly with his muzzle.

"Hi, Fly. Nice to meet you."

Fly reached out with his muzzle as well, making chomping movements once again to tell Howie that he had no ill intent, and that he knew that Howie ranked higher than he did.

"Hi, Howie. It is nice to meet you too. I am happy to be here. And I promise to behave properly," Fly said in reply to Sir Howard's welcome. Sir Howard gave him a friendly grin and tossed back his head.

"Hee-hee, you sure are polite and serious. I think I'll need to teach you a little cheerfulness, hee-hee. But go ahead and say hi to our sweet Lisa and Scamp, our little bundle of fun."

Lisa was the cautious and reserved type. She had been standing in the background watching with interest, her ears pointing forward. She made sure she was always between Scamp and the others in case of any trouble. Now that she was sure the others had taken care of vetting Fly, she was ready to say hello as well.

Carefully, she took one step toward Fly. Fly picked up on Lisa's interest and reached his neck out toward her and sniffed.

"Hi!" he said brightly, "You must be Lisa, and the little guy behind you must be Scamp. Am I right?"

Lisa reached out her neck and sniffed.

"Yes, you're right," she answered in her calm and pleasant voice, "And we want to welcome you. I hope you settle in comfortably. You look a little ragged. It will be good for you to get some proper food and care."

"Thank you, Lisa. I sure won't be worse off than I was where I came from; all of you seem very nice," Fly said eagerly.

"Fly, Fly …" someone called. "Will you play with me, will you?"

It was Scamp, who now thought that it was time to be done with all the serious business and get on with doing something active.

Lisa gave Fly an awkward look.

"I'm so sorry, Fly, but he is still very young; he has a lot to learn. I hope you will bear with him," she said.

"Yes, of course I will. I remember how boring it was when the grownups had boring get-togethers," Fly said, laughing. He carefully stepped closer to Scamp. Scamp immediately started making chomping movements with his neck stretched and his head down. Even so, he got insecure when Fly got closer, but he knew that he wouldn't be attacked as long as he was chomping.

"Hi, little guy. Just take it easy, I won't hurt you. I would like to play with you, but it must wait a little while. I am terribly hungry and thirsty. When we take a break, I promise to play with you," he said kindly.

When everybody had calmed down, it was time to continue grazing. They stuck their muzzles into the juicy green grass. Feeling safe and satisfied, they munched to their hearts' content. And boy had Fly ever missed this!

Now, it would just take time for his body and soul to feel better. Flying High became so damaged by his treatment on the racetrack. Would he ever function among humans? Perhaps with love, care, and understanding, these humans could give him a good life.

CHAPTER 17
Home of Love Farm, **Paradise**

Alice and Jacob had lived at their farm, _Home of Love_, for 17 years. They purchased the idyllic little farm when they were just married, and they loved their own little piece of heaven on earth.

Unfortunately, they never succeeded in having children, although they wanted to very much, and they both loved children so. Instead, they had decided to pour out all their love on the animals, until they were lucky enough to become foster parents for Nicholas.

When Fly arrived at _Home of Love_, he soon met the rest of the farm. In addition to the horses there were four little cats, Liv, Caja, Ziggy, and Mille, eleven hens and one rooster, as well as the dog, Benji, an Australian Shepherd/ Golden Retriever cross. He was kind, wise and curious about everything.

Benji moved in with Alice and Jacob along with Nicholas. They had lived there for almost a year.

Before that, Benji and Nicholas had lived with Nicholas' grandmother, Ella, in a little house in town. They often got fruit and vegetables, and occasionally eggs as well, from Alice and Jacob. Nicholas enjoyed visiting _Home of Love_, where he helped take care of the animals. He often spent hours watching the horses as they grazed in the pasture. He loved the horses very much. He thought they were the most wonderful creatures in the world. So beautiful, so strong, so smart, so funny, yet so delicate. They were his favorite animals.

The horses thought it was nice when Nicholas was with them. He had such a lovely personality – calm, loving, and caring. They sensed it immediately, and when he came in and sat down on the little tree stump in the pasture, they all came over to say hi to him before continuing with their activities, which were either eating, resting, playing, and rubbing on each other.

Usually, Benji joined Nicholas for his visits with the horses. With help from Jacob and Nicholas, Benji and the horses had become used to each other.

Grandma Ella was Nicholas' only relative. His parents had been killed in a traffic accident, where he got a traumatic brain injury at just two years of age. Even though he had seen pictures of his mom and dad, he didn't remember them. He only knew life with his grandmother, whom he loved more than anything in the world.

It was a terrible blow to him when she was hospitalized last year, and the doctors couldn't save her. In a way, it was good that she wasn't sick for long before she died. It would have been very hard for Nicholas to take care of his grandmother if she was ill, but it was also a big shock to him when she died so suddenly. What would happen to him now? He was only 16 years old, and he had nobody else in the whole world. Because of his brain damage, he couldn't have a regular job.

Fortunately, arrangements were made for Nicholas, and of course Benji, to live with Alice and Jacob and they were soon approved as foster parents for Nicholas.

On the *Home of Love* farm, they had a large kitchen garden, where Alice grew delicious vegetables and fruit. Jacob and Nicholas often helped in the garden when there was extra work to be done. They grew produce, both for themselves and the animals, and for friends and family. There were so many apple trees, that there were apples all year for the horses and for the eleven hens and the rooster, in addition to all the apples they ate and preserved themselves. There were long rows of carrots, which the horses also enjoyed year-round. In addition, they grew various kinds of lettuce, kale, herbs, beets, peas, leeks, and lots of other delicious things. Alice also had a patch filled with the loveliest flowers in many different colors. She loved flowers.

CHAPTER 18

A Dangerous Encounter

Every morning around 8 am, Jacob, Nicholas, and Benji would take their morning walk around the farm to feed and tend to the animals. When they reached the field, Benji ran excitedly into the pasture to say hi to the horses, one at a time, briefly touching his nose to each of their muzzles. The horses thought it was a fun game, and they loved that cute, silly dog. It doesn't happen naturally in the wild that horses and dogs become good friends. The dog is a predator that can fell and kill a horse but, with the help of a human they can easily become good friends.

The first time Benji came bounding into Fly's pasture it scared him; Fly regarded the dog as enemy number one. Benji ran straight towards Alexandra. Fly jerked up his head in fear.

"Ruuunnn!" he yelled at the top of his lungs. He spun around and rushed off at a wild gallop with large, fearful eyes and his heart pounding in his chest.

We need to hurry up and get away before they catch us! He thought, scared, while he galloped away from the horrible predator faster and faster.

When Fly reached the other end of the pasture, he stopped, huffing and puffing, and looked back in fear. He was shaking all over his body and had his eyes opened wide in confusion, when he realized that none of the others had run along with him. He saw that they were all standing at the gate, apparently having survived. He was very confused.

"Hurry up and run! You will get eaten! It's the world's most dangerous animal!" he yelled.

The others looked down at him, and Alexandra tried to calm him down.

"Don't be afraid, dear Fly. It's just Benji, he's our friend."

"But … how is it possible?" Fly asked, horrified.

"We have learned from Jacob that we can easily be good friends with Benji, even though we are so different, and we have no reason not to believe Jacob. He has never been anything but good and sweet to us," Alexandra explained.

She went down to Fly to calm him down and bring him back to the rest of the group. As leader, it was her job to keep them together and make sure everyone was okay.

Fly let her talk him into returning to the others.

"Are you sure it's not dangerous?" he asked when they got closer to Benji. Alexandra laughed good-naturedly and reassured him that Benji was completely harmless, in fact, helped look after them. He was a shepherd dog; born to protect the herd he had been tasked to by his humans.

Although Fly was almost convinced that there was no danger, he was still a little skeptical.

If I go in between the others, I'll be somewhat protected by them. Then it might be okay.

Benji was aware that Fly was new to the string, and he sensed his fear clearly. However, it was important that Fly not be scared of him so he could protect him.

Benji did exactly the right thing when he laid down in the grass with his side to Fly and placed his head on his front paws. It was a signal to Fly that he was not hunting, and it was an invitation to come closer. With his nostrils wide and sniffing, Fly approached Benji step by step.

When he was so close that the soft hairs on his muzzle touched Benji, he jumped back a step, huffing loudly.

"Yuck, it stinks," he squealed with a tight expression on his face.

The others started laughing their heads off over Fly's reaction.

"Sorry we're laughing but we all felt the same way at first. Now we're used to Benji smelling like that, and it's no longer unpleasant," Lisa said, still laughing.

"I don't even notice Benji's smell. He is so cute and funny when we play together," added little Scamp.

Scamp and Benji used to play tag every morning after touching their muzzle and nose together. They took turns running after each other until they were out of breath and agreed with almost invisible body language that they had won an equal number of times.

"Do you want to see how we play?" he asked Fly.

"Um, sure, I guess I do," Fly answered with some hesitation.

Scamp went over to Benji, who was still laying in the grass. He nudged him gently with his soft muzzle. Benji understood that the atmosphere was a little lighter, and he was ready for his morning play session with Scamp so, when Scamp spun around on his long, thin hind legs and sprinted off in a full gallop, Benji jumped up and ran headlong after him. Suddenly, Benji stopped and stood with his side facing Scamp. This made Scamp stop pretending to flee. Benji gave Scamp a quick glance and started to run away from him. This made Scamp run after Benji with a cheerful gleam in his eye.

Scamp loved their little game. He was so happy that Benji wanted to play, because the adult horses didn't really feel like playing with him. It was only Sir Howard on occasion, yet he was so old that it wasn't that fun anyway.

The two friends continued playing tag for a bit longer, while the others laughed at their funny antics. Fly looked on with wide eyes, wildly surprised at what he was seeing.

It is just like when I played with my friends in the pastures, he thought to himself.

He was suddenly brought back to the times when he and

the other foals would run around and play and have fun. He heaved a little sigh, and he became sad and downhearted by the thought of all his friends, as he felt how much he missed them.

Sir Howard noticed Fly sighing, and it made him sad. "What's wrong, little Fly?" he asked with worry.

"Oh, I just remembered all my friends. I wonder where they are now. I miss them terribly."

Fly hung his head in discouragement.

Sir Howard went over to Fly, placed his muzzle on his back for a moment, and started to rub him near his mane. It was an invitation to have a nice moment with Sir Howard, where they groomed one another in a gesture of friendship. Sir Howard was hoping it would bring Fly out of his sad thoughts; it worked.

Their friendly little moment had also made Fly more relaxed, so when Benji and Scamp were done playing and returned to the others, Fly was ready to get a little better acquainted with Benji. After all, he could see that Scamp hadn't been eaten, but that they had fun, and Fly would like that too. He really missed having fun after his horrible time at the racetrack.

When Fly approached Benji, he was approaching a friendship that would turn out to be a strong and wonderful friendship to last the rest of their lives.

It had been two weeks since Flying High came home to Alice, Jacob, Nicholas, and all their animals at the farm. The other horses had received him so well and given him so much care and love that he soon was content and happy with them in the big pasture.

Yet still, every time the atmosphere around Fly changed, he became fearful and anxious. Fortunately, their pasture was on the other side of the farm, and it was quite peaceful. So, by and large, Fly was doing very well and had become accustomed to the daily routine at the farm. Even though he participated often in Scamp's and Benji's game of tag, he kept his distance to both Jacob and Nicholas, keeping a sharp eye on them and on everything they did when they were in the pasture.

Fly could see clearly that the other horses liked being with them.

"They are really very nice to us," Alexandra tried to tell Fly over and over but Fly just felt an intense anxiety fill his entire body every time they got close to him. His heart would beat fast, and he would feel a compelling urge to run away. Even though they brought delicious apples and carrots, Fly wouldn't eat them until they left again.

"Do you see how scared he is?" Jacob asked Nicholas on this particular morning.

"Not really!" he responded.

"Try looking at his eyes. They are wide open and perfectly round, and you can see a little of the white in his eye that normally is not visible."

"Oh, yeah, I see that!" Nicholas said.

"Then you also see that there are some wrinkles around, and especially above, his eye, right?"

Nicholas could see that too.

"Am I right that his nostrils are pinched shut a little, and that he is tight around his muzzle?" Nicholas asked.

"Yep! Good job noticing that! Do you also see the way the ears are turning back and forth all the time?"

"Yeah! It looks funny," Nicholas smiled.

"You're right, but it's also a sign that he is very alert to all the sounds around him. Horses have even better hearing than humans. This is because their ears are shaped like funnels, so sounds enter more easily and clearly, and because they can turn their ears in every direction, they can figure out in a split second precisely where the sounds are coming from. They don't even have to turn their heads like we do," Jacob explained.

"That's really smart ... a movable ear funnel! It's also like his whole body is stiff and ready to run. A little like he is waiting for someone to say *one, two, three, run*," Nicholas said.

"You have become very good at understanding the horses, Nico! I am proud of you, son!"

Nicholas beamed with pride at Jacob's praise. He had called him "son". They stood in silence watching Fly who looked back at them.

"When he stands with his head high like he does now, it is also a sign that he is on alert. When he holds his head that high, he can see far and clearly," Jacob explained.

"Whoops!" Nicholas suddenly exclaimed, laughing, "he lost his halter!"

"Well, he sure did," Jacob answered with a chuckle, "We'd better find it before one of them gets it tangled around a leg."

Jacob and Nicholas started to walk around the pasture to look for Fly's halter. They walked around quietly chatting while looking at the ground. They weren't thinking about it, but it was actually a very good thing to do in terms of getting Fly used to their presence in the pasture. If Jacob had thought about it more, he already knew that. It was one of the main theories behind horse training: that moving around with your gaze lowered, relaxed shoulders, and with your side or back to the horse, you are displaying non-threatening behavior.

"There it is!" Nicholas exclaimed excitedly, pointing as he spotted the red halter lying in the grass. Jacob walked over and picked it up. It wasn't broken, so he wondered how it had come off Fly.

"Hmm, I wonder if Howie pulled it off while they were playing," said Jacob.

"That might very well be!" Nicholas said with a laugh. "That Howie is quite a trickster, and he is strong enough, so he could easily pull it off Fly."

While they were searching for the halter, Fly had been

standing still as a statue, looking at them.

I wonder what they are doing, he thought, looking on with wide, attentive eyes and his head lifted high.

They are carnivores, after all, so why are they walking around looking at the grass?

He was completely confused, and he began to step around himself a little with his tail lifted high, while he made huffing sounds in an attempt to sniff his way to the answer. He couldn't do it, but he noticed that they weren't coming *toward* him, but rather walking back and forth, further and further *away* from him. He could hear them making strange sounds with their mouths, but they were calm and gentle sounds.

Fly calmed down a little and came to a stop.

Hmm, it doesn't seem like they are wanting to attack me like the humans usually do when they come into our pastures or into my box.

He remembered much too well the two times when he had been captured in the pasture and forced into a truck.

Fly turned his head and looked at the other horses, who were standing by the gate chomping on apples and carrots.

"Is it normal for them to walk around the pasture without hurting us?" he yelled to them.

Alexandra, heavy in foal, lifted her head.

"Yes, Fly. Jacob walks around here all the time to make sure everything is okay. It is not the least bit dangerous; he is simply caring for us," she said. She lowered her head and continued chomping on her treats.

Reassured by Alexandra, Fly glanced over at the humans standing with the halter before joining the other horses.

"I think we need to wait before we try to put the halter back on Fly," Jacob said. "He won't let us approach him, so we'll have to wait until he feels safer about us. Or – hopefully – realizes that he *is* safer with us," he corrected himself.

"When will you start training him?" Nicolas asked.

"We start tomorrow," Jacob said with a smile.

"Yay! I'm so excited! Fly is such a special horse. I know that with training you will help him have the best life he can have," he said earnestly.

CHAPTER 19
Can Fly be Trained?

The next day, Alice and Jacob started to train Fly. They had many years' experience training horses, and they had read and studied quite a bit about horsemanship. They liked the idea of doing things on the horse's terms and in ways the horse already understood, so it wouldn't be stressed, but rather would want to participate.

They had decided to start the training in the pasture, so Fly wouldn't have to be separated from the other horses. The first thing they wanted to do was to get Fly used to their presence in the pasture from time to time. Fly needed to feel safe about them being with him and the other horses.

"I can't wait to see how it goes today," said Alice, "I want so much for little Fly to let us help him. I've already grown to love him so much."

"I feel the same way you do, Alice. We'll need to give him plenty of time, and if we can't do it ourselves, I am willing to find someone else to help," Jacob said kindly.

Alice agreed whole-heartedly with Jacob.

Until now, they had been back by the horse pasture several times a day, just so Fly would get used to seeing them.

They were happily surprised that Fly had gotten used to Benji so quickly and even wanted to play with him.

Therefore, it was with both anticipation and optimism they started the first training day.

To avoid pressuring Fly too much, they did what they had

done every morning since Fly's arrival. They went down to the pasture and let Benji run in by the horses, while they, themselves, stayed outside the fence. Nicholas was there too. He didn't want to miss a moment of training with Fly.

Benji ran over to Alexandra first and greeted her by touching his nose to her muzzle in a little, quick movement.

"Good morning," Benji said.

"Good morning," Alexandra answered.

Then he sped over to Sir Howard, and they did the same thing, after which it was Lisa's turn to get a "morning kiss" from him.

Fly was in a playful mood this morning, so he beat Benji to it and ran over to him, nudged Benji's side with his muzzle, spun around on his strong hind legs and took off in a full gallop, tossing his head so his beautiful black mane and forelock billowed in large waves while he yelled:

"Scaaaaamp! Cooooome, let's run from Benji!"

Scamp was very perky for the early hour and took off at a gallop while taking lots of leaps, or at least trying. After all, he wasn't too sure on his long foal legs yet, but he certainly felt that he was taking *giant* leaps.

"Whoo-hoo!" he squealed, leaping and bounding.

Benji dashed after them with his tongue hanging out.

When they all had run as much as they could for a moment, Benji stopped suddenly, turned his side to the two horses and looked at them.

It was only a split second before Fly and Scamp saw that Benji had stopped. They stopped as well and spun around, and when Benji looked away and took off in the opposite direction, they took off after him, clumps of grass flying all around them.

Everyone else laughed and commented on how funny all three of them looked and that they were so silly.

Benji, Scamp, and Fly had a great time. They played a little longer, and when they didn't want to play anymore, they walked together to the watering hole to quench their thirst.

Benji loved this cozy moment when all three of them were drinking from the fresh water.

After everyone had settled back down, they went out into the middle of the pasture as a group to start their daily grazing along the route they followed every day.

Benji ran out through the fence to Alice, Jacob, and Nicholas.

"Nico, do you want a job? We need to make sure Benji stays here with you, while we work with Fly in the pasture," Jacob asked.

"Sure," he replied giving Benji a pat.

Nicholas was happy that he could help. He knew that Jacob and Alice were the ones who had to train Fly initially, but he hoped with all his heart that he would also be able to participate at some point.

Alice and Jacob walked into the pasture. They approached the string by walking in arcs toward the horses, so they constantly moved with their sides to them. They walked with their eyes down and their arms calmly at their sides, and their breathing was slow and steady. They chatted with each other to show the horses that they were not silent predators sneaking up on them.

Alexandra stopped eating, lifted her head, and looked at Alice and Jacob. Fly had registered that Alexandra was looking up. He was always extraordinarily watchful, so he lifted his head with a quick jerk and looked around frantically.

"What's going on?" he asked with a shrill voice.

"Don't worry, little Fly, you don't have any reason to be scared. It's just Alice and Jacob. They aren't dangerous!" Alexandra put her muzzle down into the juicy grass and kept grazing. Of course, she was used to the humans walking in the pasture, so she saw no reason to alarm the string. She had assessed the situation and found that all was well.

Fly, however, was not convinced. He felt uneasy and began

walking around the string, putting more distance between the humans and himself.

What do they want? Do they want to catch me and take me away?

Fly was scared. The memories welled up in him from the two other times when he had been captured in the pastures, first to be taken away from his mom, and secondly from the other young colts.

I am not going to let them catch me! I am not!

Fly felt his fear mixing with anger. He stopped, stretched out his neck, and huffed so loudly through his dilated nostrils that his beautiful chestnut body gave a start and his handsome black mane billowed in the breeze.

Alice and Jacob noticed Fly's reaction, but they figured that it was okay to continue over to the string because the other horses were completely calm, grazing as though they didn't have a care in the world.

"Howie, what's happening? Are they coming to catch me?" Fly yelled to Sir Howard.

Sir Howard lifted his head and looked at Fly. He hadn't realized how scared Fly had become. He had been busy grazing but when he saw Fly, he got worried and walked over to him.

"Don't you worry one bit, Fly. Nothing will happen to you, I promise. When Alexandra said that everything is fine and that there is no danger, then that's a fact."

"But...but," Fly stammered, "Why are they in our pasture?"

"I don't really know, but usually they are just here spending time with us. In fact, we enjoy our time with them. They scratch us a little, sometimes they bring treats," he explained.

Sir Howard looked back and let his gaze rest on Jacob and Alice. He tried to calm Fly down by telling him that these humans had never hurt any of them, but it was hard to find the right way to explain it. After all, it was a question of trust, and they still needed to earn Fly's.

Sir Howard tossed his head that meant 'come with me and I'll take care of you.' Fly hesitated but soon followed Sir Howard back to the string. He knew he was better protected when he was with the others; it was harder for an enemy to choose one among many.

Alice and Jacob watched Fly follow Sir Howard back and they immediately turned their backs to them. Slowly and quietly, they walked away from the horses, heading to the gate and out of the pasture. They did this intentionally to show Fly that when *he* moved toward *them*, they walked away from *him*. They used the "pressure and release" principle, which they knew was one of the best training methods they had.

Fly kept his eyes on them the whole time and watched as they walked away.

"Whoa, look Howie! They are leaving!"

"It's like I said, little Fly. They weren't dangerous in the least!" Sir Howard laughed heartily to lighten the mood.

"You're right!" he cheered as he tossed back his head playfully. He then leapt and bucked happily, releasing the tension he felt moments before. Fly had a vague memory of that day on the racetrack when he followed Nicholas onto the truck.

Hmmm, he thought, *something is different when the humans walk away from us.*

Fly was happy again. The two friends groomed each other affectionately.

Alice and Jacob had come out on the other side of the fence, where Benji and Nicholas had followed everything with curiosity.

"That was exciting!" Nicholas exclaimed. "How do you think it went?" he asked Alice, scratching Benji behind one ear.

"I think it went very well," Alice replied. "Obviously, I'm disappointed that Fly reacted so strongly, choosing to run from the other horses.

"It was clear that he was scared, but he calmed down quickly once good old Howie helped him. We can work with him, he will come around," she said with a smile.

"I hope he understood why we chose to walk away at the very moment we did. It will help if he understands the pressure and release principle quickly," Jacob added.

"I'm sure he did," Alice said. "After all, that's what worked at the racetrack, when Nico got him to join him in the truck. That was an incredibly good job, Nico!" she said beaming at Nicholas.

Even though they had praised Nicholas for it many times since that day, they continued; it really was amazing. He did something nobody else had been able to do with Fly, strictly by using his intuition. Nobody had taught him how to do that.

Even though he had sustained a traumatic brain injury, Nicholas was certainly not slow-witted. In fact, it seemed the injury heightened his senses; he was very empathetic and intuitive. Among other things, this meant that most animals loved his company because he had a very clear sense of them, and they could feel it.

Alice cleared her throat and gestured toward the house.

"I think we need a good breakfast. How do pancakes sound?" she asked.

"YEAH!" Nicholas and Jacob cheered at the same time. Benji, who had been lying quietly jumped up, danced around them, and wagged his tail. Even though he didn't know why everyone was suddenly so happy, he was happy too. When Benji's pack was happy, so was he.

The horses had made it far into the pasture, but they could still hear the excitement of the humans. They looked up briefly before continuing to graze on the delicious, juicy green grass.

CHAPTER 20
<u>Trust Before Anything Else</u>

Alice and Jacob decided to use the same training method with Fly for six days straight. They knew that each step had to be done very carefully with a horse as damaged and sensitive as Fly was. If you proceed too quickly, you can make the damage even worse and the trust you are trying to build can be broken forever. Therefore, they spent the next days working in the exact same way as they had on the first day.

Fly's heartrate was still high, and he was in a heightened state of alert when Alice and Jacob were in the pasture. The fear showed clearly in his big beautiful black eyes, and he kept a sharp eye on them. His entire beautiful, chestnut body was stiff and ready to flee.

Hmm, Fly thought on the third day, *I have to try to trust Alexandra and the others when they say there is no danger when Alice and Jacob are in our pasture. But I will still keep my distance and keep the other horses between us.*

Fly kept an eye on every little movement Alice and Jacob made, but they stayed on the other side of the string, satisfied with the fact that Fly hadn't run off in a panic like he did the first two days.

"Let's just stay here for a little while and move slowly with the horses as they graze," Jacob said. Alice thought it was a good idea. They chatted as they meandered along with the horses on the opposite side of where Fly was.

"Jacob, how many days do you think is left before

Alexandra will be foaling?"

"It will probably happen in a couple of days. She has collapsed a bit above her tail, and she looks a little open in her rear. I want to check if the teats are waxing."

Alexandra was standing right next to them, so Jacob went down alongside her and bent over slowly, so he could see her udder.

"It is starting to swell, all right, but there is no waxing," he said.

"The due date will probably hold. She is an amazing broodmare. She got pregnant easily, so her foaling will probably be easy as well. I think she will be a great mom," said Alice.

"You are so right," Jacob laughed. "Even though it's hard to wait for the new little wonder, we will have to be patient."

Fly had seen and heard everything that happened. He had slowly calmed down a little, but he still chose to keep an eye on Alice and Jacob. He was still too anxious and tense to eat like the other horses.

"When are they leaving again?" Fly asked the other horses. He was hungry as he had dropped his stomach contents earlier, so he would weigh as little as possible in case he needed to flee.

Sir Howard, who stood the closest, looked at Fly.

"It probably won't be long, little Fly," he said reassuringly. "I am really proud of you for staying with us today instead of running away when they came."

"Thanks, Howie, but I'm still so scared. I can't sense or feel what they want. So, I prefer to stay as far away as possible, while still having the safety of being with the rest of you," he said. His voice was tense and a little shaky.

Sir Howard again tried to explain to Fly that the humans were trying to show they didn't want to harm him. They wanted so much for Fly to come to trust them. By having trust in those around you, you can live a life in peace and harmony. When you live in peace and harmony, it is easier to tackle the challenges you encounter in the world.

Fly heard what Sir Howard said, but he couldn't begin to imagine having trust in the humans after everything they had done to him. He didn't understand them, and in his experience, they didn't understand him either. The anxiety and fear he had of them was so deep and strong that it surfaced every time the humans were near.

Suddenly, Fly lifted his head even higher. He had noticed that Alice and Jacob had turned their backs to the string and were starting to move away slowly and calmly, as they kept their shoulders relaxed and low. Fly followed them with a sharp eye, still on alert.

What are they doing now? he thought.

He paced back and forth, a little uneasy, but he kept his anxiety at bay and managed to stay with the string.

Once Alice and Jacob had left the enclosure, Fly took a deep breath, relaxed his tense muscles, and started to graze next to Sir Howard.

Nicholas and Benji were waiting outside the enclosure. Nicholas had followed everything with curiosity and excitement – he didn't want to miss a single moment of Fly's training.

"How did it go?" he asked.

He thought Fly had done a really good job today. It was huge that he stayed with the string, but he didn't know if Alice and Jacob thought it was good enough.

"It went very well today, Nico. Fly stayed with the string. That's big progress considering the state he's in," Alice replied.

"Yes," Jacob added, "It went very well though it still hurts my heart to see how scared Fly is."

"I just can't wait until we can get close enough to him to give him lots of hugs and tell him how much we love him," Nicholas said in an eager voice.

Alice and Jacob laughed heartily. Jacob gave Nicholas a hug.

"I love you to the moon and back, Nico, and I love that you love the animals just as much as we do. I am forever grateful for you and Benji being here with us," he said warmly.

Joy and happiness bubbled up inside Nicholas, and a big smile spread on his friendly face.

"Come, Benji! Let's race to the house!" he called with a cheerful voice.

Benji was ready. He jumped up in excitement, spun around himself several times, wagged his tail and took off with Nicholas.

"Come on, Benji, last one in is a rotten egg!" he called behind him.

Alice and Jacob laughed loudly and followed them up to the house. It was time for a cup of morning coffee.

The cats, Liv, Caja, Ziggy, and Mille were waiting for them at the front door, ready to have breakfast served as they had it every morning. After their coffee, Alice and Nicholas would go to the chicken coop to collect eggs, while Jacob went out to work in the vegetable patch.

CHAPTER 21

A New Plan

The sixth training day had arrived. Alice, Jacob, and Nicholas were talking about how they would approach their work with Fly today. The last couple of days hadn't made much of a difference and they worried about whether they could handle the task.

Fly did indeed stay with the string when they entered the pasture, but he didn't eat while they were there. He was still uneasy when they moved. He continued to keep to the other side of the string, occasionally huffing loudly, keeping a sharp eye on them.

Jacob looked at Alice and Nico.

"Do you have any suggestions as to what we can do differently today?" he asked the two.

"Maybe it would make a difference for Fly if just one of you went in there," Nicholas said.

"Nico! That's a great idea!" Alice exclaimed, "That might help take some pressure off Fly".

"Nico, you're on to something there. I think we should try it! High five!" Jacob said.

Their praise thrilled Nico, and he felt proud to be able to contribute to Fly's training.

"You often see that horses are more fearful of men than of women and children. I think Alice should go into the pasture today," Jacob said, "What do you think about that?"

"I like it," Alice replied, "It makes a lot of sense considering the fact that only men were trying to train Fly at the racetrack."

"How can horses tell the difference between men, women, and children?" Nicholas asked, tilting his head quizzically at Jacob and Alice.

"Hmm, that's a great question, Nico. I never actually thought about why it's that way," Alice said. "Do you know, Jacob?"

"Off-hand, there is no scientific proof that horses can actually tell the difference, but many horse owners find that their horses react differently to men, women, and children," Jacob explained. "I think that if horses have been treated like Fly has been treated, and only men were cruel, then the horse probably associates that with men's scent, voice tone, size, movements, and other differences."

Nicholas' face turned pensive.

"I knew a pony that feared children. It walked alone in a field near the school. I noticed that when children came around, it would hurry up and run away, but if only grownups came by, it just looked at them and kept doing what it was doing. I wonder why that was."

Alice thought about it for a minute.

"It might be because some kids had teased it or even been mean to it on their way to and from school. Of course, there might be other reasons, but if it had been there for a long time, then that might be what happened."

"That makes a lot of sense!" Nico furrowed his brown and tilted his head. "Now that I think about it, I remember that some boys threw rocks at the poor pony. They yelled and jeered at it while they laughed viciously. Fortunately, there was an adult who found out about it and took care of it, but after that happened, it was always scared of kids; even the ones that didn't do anything to it."

Alice put an arm around Nicholas' shoulder and gave him a squeeze.

"Good thing the adults took care of it, but poor little pony.

It saw it as though children attacked it and were dangerous creatures that wanted to do it harm. That's why it would flee, the first reaction of a horse is to flee if it can. Fortunately, that pony could," she said.

CHAPTER 22

A Foal is Born

The next day with the new plan ready, Alice, Jacob, Nicholas, and Benji went down to the horses in the pasture. On the way, Nico and Benji were playing tag around Alice and Jacob, who laughed heartily as Nico and Benji played.

When they were a few yards from the enclosure, Benji stopped suddenly. He froze and bristled, as he bared his teeth and growled. He had been the first to see that a change had taken place in the string. Nico saw Benji's reaction, stopped, and looked over at the horses.

"Look, look, look right there!" he cheered excitedly while pointing eagerly. "There's a new foal! Alexandra had her baby!"

He jumped up and down at the sight of a little dark brown foal on its wobbly, long foal legs. Alice turned and looked to the pasture.

"My God, Jacob, the foal has arrived!" she gasped.

Alice joined Nico in pointing eagerly toward the little newborn.

"No way!" Jacob exclaimed. "It sure has! It's beautiful."

"I can't wait to see if it's a filly or a colt. What do you guys think it is?" Alice asked, "I think it's a girl."

"Do you want to make a bet?" Jacob asked.

Nicholas thought that was a fun idea. "What should we bet?"

"A *huge* hug from the losers?" Jacob replied. Both

Nicholas and Alice were game for that.

"Hmm, Alice thinks it's a girl, but I think it's a boy," Jacob said.

"I think so too," Nicholas chimed in.

Now he couldn't wait to find out which one of them would win the bet.

"I'm looking forward to getting *huge* hugs from you two scoundrels," Alice said, laughing.

Benji had calmed down when he saw the rest of them acting relaxed.

Inside the pasture, the horses had had an uneasy night, and they were tired. When Alexandra had started her contractions and the delivery had begun, she had looked at Sir Howard and tossed her head in the direction of the other horses.

"Howie, you need to be my stand-in and take good care of the others. I am going to go over here a little way, and I will be back after the delivery."

Sir Howard lowered his head, stretched his neck, and lifted his head again in one smooth movement.

"Of course, Alexandra. Don't you worry one bit – I will do my very best to take care of all of them!"

Sir Howard gave Alexandra a little nudge to the back of one thigh, turned around, and went over to the other horses, who had stayed a little in the background.

They knew that something was afoot but Scamp and Fly were a little anxious, since they didn't know if something good or bad was about to happen.

Lisa calmed them with her gentle voice.

"My little friends, don't you worry. Nothing will happen. Alexandra is coming back in at little while. She just needs a little peace while she foals."

Scamp and Fly didn't know what foaling was, but they let Lisa calm them down. Of course, she would never subject Scamp to danger, so when she said things were okay, then things were okay! Scamp had gotten hungry, so he took his place next to Lisa and started nudging her udder. The milk began to flow, and he nursed with loud, satisfied slurps.

For the next hour or so, they could hear Alexandra make different sounds. It scared them a little, because they could hear that it wasn't very comfortable for her.

After some time, those sounds gave way to completely different ones. They could hear little grunting sounds and the sound of Alexandra licking; she was done foaling, and it had gone very well. Her new little foal was just perfect. It was a dark brown filly with a beautiful star marking and white socks on her forelegs.

Now, Alexandra just had to lick her until she was clean and dry, then it was all about her getting to her feet as soon as possible. Mother and daughter had already gotten to know each other's scents and sounds; it's an instinct that ensures that the horses can always find each other.

Even though it was Alexandra's first foal, she knew precisely what she should do. Instinctively, she waited for the foal to stand up by herself. She wouldn't help unless it was necessary. The foal would learn best by doing things for herself and in her own way.

The foal's instinct quickly prompted her to start trying to get up on her long, wobbly legs. She was an alert and perky little thing, so after a few tries she succeeded at standing. She started looking for her mother's udder. She was fast at finding that too, and when she started to push and suck on the udder, Alexandra let out a couple of squeals in surprise as her udder let down the milk.

Alexandra and her newborn soon rejoined the string. The others were terribly curious about seeing the little new one, but Alexandra made sure she stayed between her foal and the other horses, protectively. The others were allowed to look but not touch, at least not yet.

When Fly saw the foal for the first time, it evoked strong feelings in him. After all, he was born with great leadership qualities, and among other things this meant that he was quick at gaining an overview. He sensed immediately that the foal was a valuable member of the string.

Oh! He thought, *that's what Alexandra was doing, and that is what a foal is. There is one more of us now, and that's good for our chances of survival!*

"Now, I understand better why you were so somber and a little uneasy, Howie, this is a big event," Fly said.

"Yes, when we get new family members many things can go wrong. Fortunately, it goes well most of the time, and today it did too."

Sir Howard was visibly relieved, and his voice was regaining the light tone it normally had. He was happy that Alexandra was back, and that she had reassumed her leadership position. It is a big responsibility to be leader of the string, and even though Sir Howard was pretty good at it, he wasn't quite good enough to be the leader for an extended period.

The rest of the night, everyone was a little more alert than usual, keeping an eye on their surroundings and the little newcomer, while they grazed and rested as they always did.

The next morning Alexandra was the first to notice that their group of humans had arrived, as usual. When she looked at them, the others saw them too. Her little foal was frightened by these beings, whom she had never seen.

Alexandra reassured her by placing herself between the foal and Alice, Jacob, Nicholas, and Benji.

"Don't be afraid. If you stay with me and do what I tell you, I can protect you. I won't let anything bad happen to you," she told her little one.

Alice and Jacob had entered the pasture. When they approached the string, Alexandra came to meet them. She loved her humans and was proud of her newborn filly; she couldn't wait to show her off.

The foal was anxious, but also very curious. She lowered her head to look at the strangers from under her mom's belly.

Alexandra laughed and turned around.

"Don't worry one bit, honey. These humans are our friends. They are nice and they care for us," she said.

Alexandra used her muzzle to give the foal a loving nudge in the general direction of Alice and Jacob, who were standing there mesmerized, looking in excitement at that perfect little foal.

Alice was deeply touched, and her voice was thick.

"Oh, Alexandra, she is wonderful! Thank you so much for bringing her into this world, you must be so proud," she said softly.

Alice put hand over her mouth, tears welling up in her eyes; how was it possible for nature to create something this dainty, perfect, and altogether beautiful.

Jacob was moved as well.

"Congratulations, Alexandra! What a great job! What a wonder you have created," he said with a bit of a lump in his throat. He squatted and looked under Alexandra's belly at the foal.

"It's a little filly! Alice, it's a girl!" he exclaimed.

"Yay! You and Nico owe me some big hugs!" Alice said with a laugh.

"That's right," Jacob laughed. "You won the bet!"

Jacob had gotten back up and wrapped his arms around Alice. He gave her a huge bearhug and a big wet kiss. He was so happy and proud of his family – both the humans and the animals.

Alice hugged Jacob back and gave him a big kiss too. Love filled her heart and joy washed over her. Moments like these brought meaning to life, she thought.

"I love you so much, Jacob, and everything we have together. Maybe there are better things and more beautiful places, but I wouldn't trade what we have for anything in the world!" she said looking into her husband's eyes.

They both looked at the foal a little longer before turning around and walking back to Nicholas and Benji.

"How about we let Nico name the little newcomer?" Jacob asked.

"That's an amazing idea," Alice said. "He'll be so proud to have that honor."

Nicholas was bursting with curiosity as he waited to find out if it was a filly or a colt, but he knew it would scare the horses if he yelled to Jacob and Alice, so he waited quietly for their return.

"What is it?" he asked eagerly. "Do you owe Alice a giant hug?"

Nicholas giggled. A broad smile spread across Jacob's face.

"Oh! So, it's a filly! We'll have another mare who can hand down Alexandra's good genes in the next generation!" he exclaimed.

He gave Alice her winning hug, and of course he got one in return.

"You're right, Nico. It's important to breed with good genes to improve the chances of healthy and strong horses," she said.

"Not to change the subject," Jacob interjected, "... but don't you think it's better if we give the horses a day of peace and quiet and save Fly's training for tomorrow?"

Both Alice and Nicholas thought that was a good idea.

"I think we should drop Benji playing with them today as well. I'm afraid it will scare the little foal," Nicholas said.

Jacob beamed at Nicholas, the pride in his voice was unmistakable.

"Nico, I'm so proud of you for demonstrating good horsemanship by thinking that way. By the way, we have decided that you should name the foal," he said smiling.

"Really?! Awesome! Thank you!" he exclaimed.

Nicholas danced around with excitement, making funny jumps and leaps. As usual, Benji joined him in his celebratory antics.

Alice and Jacob laughed heartily.

Nicholas thought as hard as he could as they walked back toward the farm.

"Aphrodite!" he suddenly exclaimed. "I think her name should be Aphrodite! What do you think about that? I remember that Aphrodite is the name of a goddess, who is known for being the goddess of love, beauty, and fertility. I think that's a beautiful name for a future broodmare."

"That's *really* beautiful – it's just the right name for the little beauty," Jacob said with a smile.

Now, their daily chores awaited them. They loved every one of them; it was part of creating the life they loved living on their little farm.

CHAPTER 23
That Didn't Go So Well!

The next morning, everything was peaceful and idyllic when Alice, Jacob, Nicholas, and Benji got down to the horses in the pasture. It was the day when Alice would go into the pasture alone. If she didn't make any progress today, they would bring in another horse trainer. They would not give up on Fly.

Fly was in dire need of a farrier, and that was completely out of the question if they couldn't even catch him! Over breakfast, they had discussed what Alice should do during training today with the understanding that improvisation may be necessary.

The plan was simple: they wouldn't let Benji do his morning ritual with the horses, because he had yet to be introduced to Aphrodite. They would save that for after the training, or perhaps for the next day.

Alice would walk into the pasture in the same way she and Jacob had done the other days. She would approach the string from the opposite side of where Fly was. She would walk calmly with her shoulders low and approach them sideways.

The others would keep a keen eye on Fly's reactions.

If Fly stayed with the string without getting too uneasy while Alice was on the other side of them, Alice would move slowly from horse to horse and talk to each one calmly. She would talk to them in a soft, calm voice and use so-called "calming" words. Words like the word *good* or words she could say slowly like *ni-i-i-i-ice*, or *hi-i-i-i-i-i*. Alice would take her time with it, even if it took an hour to get to the horse standing closest to Fly.

The goal was for Fly to stay with the string and relax enough to eat grass while Alice was among them.

They were all very excited, but Alice took a few deep breaths to calm her pulse and relax her body completely.

"I'm ready," she said.

"We will tell you how he reacts, so you don't need to make eye contact with him," Jacob said.

"Yes," Nicholas chimed in. "We will keep a good eye on him."

As usual, Alexandra was the first to discover that her humans had arrived. She stopped grazing, lifted her head to look at them. Gauging that everything was okay, she continued to graze.

The night had gone well, and little Aphrodite drank milk, slept, and played; precisely as a newborn foal should.

As always, Fly was on alert.

Even though he knew that Alexandra took care of all of them, he kept an extra eye on his surroundings. It was stressful and exhausting for him, but his experience with the humans had filled him with so much anxiety and unease that he was ready to flee at the slightest sign of danger. He had seen them come as well, and when he saw Alice go into the pasture, he stopped eating and followed her with a sharp eye.

"Why can't they just leave us alone?" he asked the others. Lisa stood closest to him.

"Sweet Fly. I completely understand that it's hard to grasp, but they are nice, and they are our friends. Sometimes they do things with us and for us. At times they need us to come with them." Lisa stopped. She found that it was hard to explain after all. "You can stay by me, if you want, little Fly." She gave Fly a gentle nudge to the shoulder and kept grazing after having observed that Scamp was doing great with Sir Howard.

Fly quickly moved his gaze from Alice to Lisa and back again.

"I don't understand what you mean. But thanks for your help, Lisa."

Fly was uneasy, but he stayed with Lisa, while he kept an eye on Alice.

I see no reason at all why I should let them come over to me. So, I'll just stay here till she goes away again.

Alice worked with a lot of patience and with the calmest body language. She moved from Alexandra and Aphrodite, who stayed on the opposite side of her mother, to Sir Howard and to Scamp. She spoke calmly with each horse individually, petting each of them slowly.

All the horses enjoyed it fully. They loved Alice, and it was nice when she petted them. She knew her horses very well, and she knew precisely where each individual one preferred to be scratched.

Now, Alice started to approach Lisa, which was the horse that was closest to Fly. Until now, Fly had made no progress compared to the other days. But at least it hadn't gotten worse.

When Fly saw Alice move away from Scamp in the direction of Lisa and consequently himself, his heart started to pound violently. He froze momentarily with wide, fearful eyes, before spinning around with so much force that clumps of grass flew from his hoofs as he took off at a wild gallop down the pasture.

It all happened so quickly that neither Alice, Jacob, Nicholas, or any of the other horses had time to react and interfere before Fly was a good distance away.

"Oh, no," Alice sighed sadly. She continued talking to no one in particular.

"Poor Fly. I feel so sorry for him. It hurts me when I see

how scared he is. What he's been through must have been horrible!"

Tears were now streaming down Alice's cheeks as she walked back slowly to Jacob, Nicholas, and Benji. She quickly wiped her eyes and cheeks so Nicholas wouldn't see that she was sad, but she was so affected emotionally that the others noticed immediately. They didn't say anything, but they gave her a big hug, and they stood for a while holding each other, all three of them.

Benji sat looking at them. He cocked his head and whined a little before getting up, walking over to them, and pressing himself against one of Alice's legs. He didn't know what was wrong, but he had a clear sense his humans were sad. So, he offered comfort and help.

"You did a great job, Alice!" Jacob said. "We have done all we can but Fly needs more help than we can give him."

Alice let out a little sniffle.

"Thanks, Jacob. And thank you, Nico and Benji."

She bent over and gave Benji a friendly pat on the back.

"We all did our best, but we have a lot to learn before we can work with a horse as damaged as Fly," she said sadly.

Fly had seen Alice leave, so he returned to his friends. When he saw the humans starting to walk back toward the farm, he heaved a deep sigh, huffed and yawned to release the tension from his body, before he started to eat alongside the others.

The decision was made.

Flying High needed more help. They had to find someone who could do it, but it had to be someone with the same approach to horse training that they had themselves.

CHAPTER 24
Nightmare

The snake was huge! It was extraordinarily long and very thick. The color was dark brown to the point of being nearly black!

Fly was sweating foam.

Desperate and scared to death, he jumped from corner to corner in the tiny room where he was imprisoned.

"Heeeelp, heeeelp, heeeelp!" he screamed at the top of his lungs.

With the fear burning in his black eyes and the scent of the creepy and dangerous snake in his dilated nostrils, Fly was unable to think a single cohesive thought.

He couldn't flee, and the snake kept attacking him. The snake laid down on the floor, after which it opened its giant mouth filled with needle sharp teeth and threw its long, thick, dark body against Fly at a speed he would never have thought possible.

Fortunately, the snake kept missing him every time it slammed shut its giant mouth.

But how long before Fly ran out of strength to throw himself out of reach of its violent attacks?

What could he do?

Why was nobody coming to help him?

"Wake up, Fly, wake up!" Sir Howard called as he nudged Fly who was sleeping completely flat and stretched out on the ground.

Fly made some sniffing and huffing sounds, and his legs were kicking off and on like he was preparing to run.

Sir Howard nudged Fly a few more times.

Suddenly, and with a big start, Fly lifted his head from the ground and jumped up like the ground under him was on fire. He was trembling all over his body. Desperate, he turned his head from side to side, his beautiful mane and forelock formed a black cascade around him. He stood as on pins and needles, ready to flee, but he didn't know which direction he should run. Because where did the snake go?

Sir Howard had been frightened enough by Fly's intense reaction to jump a step to the side.

"Wow! You sure have fast legs, Fly! What happened?" he asked.

"Where is the snake, Howie? Where is it?" Fly asked in a shrill and trembling voice.

Fear radiated from every square inch of his beautiful chestnut body and from the gorgeous black eyes, as he stood tight as a bow, ready to flee.

"Ehm, what snake?" Sir Howard asked, giving Fly a puzzled look before he realized that Fly must have had a nightmare.

"Oh, you poor little thing! There is no snake. I think you had another one of those nightmares."

"Whoa, that makes me feel better. But I'm telling you, Howie, it was the biggest, fastest, most lethal and horrifying snake I have yet experienced in my dreams. Why do I keep dreaming about snakes that want to kill me?" Fly asked with a sad little voice.

"I don't know, but perhaps because you have had an experience with snakes or with something related to snakes. And if you are still holding onto it, it can trigger bad dreams, or it can mean that you will be scared if you experience something that reminds you."

"You're so wise, Howie, a snake bit me once; it hurt for several days. Also, at the racetrack, they would often throw long snakes at me and on me when they wanted to capture me in the box. It made me so scared that I could barely breathe. And it's not like I could run away."

By now, Fly was almost calm. He was standing exhausted next to Sir Howard with his head down.

Perhaps it was the experience with Alice today that triggered the bad dream. I got scared and ran away. It is true what Howie says? That after something happens that makes me scared, I often have nightmares. I wonder if it will ever stop.

CHAPTER 25
<u>Sofia</u>

The next morning the family sat around the breakfast table.

"I actually saw an article in the weekly news the other day about a horse whisperer," Alice said. She got up and went into the living room to get the paper.

"Here it is!" Her eyes lit up with excitement as she looked at the photo accompanying the article.

It showed a little blond, younger woman and a beautiful bright white horse. The woman and the horse were together inside a rotunda, a round enclosure, and there were people outside looking at them. The horse was standing relaxed with its head lowered in front of the woman, and the woman held one hand on the forehead of the horse.

Alice started to read the article aloud for Jacob and Nicholas. It turned out that the woman lived nearby, and it said she worked with most types of problems with horses.

"What's her name…Let me see if it says …" Alice hummed softly, while she skimmed through the text to find a name.

"Yep, it says here. Her name is Sofia! Buuuuut … there is no phone number or other contact information."

"It is often that way with newspaper articles," Jacob said. "But I think that she's the one who has helped Peter and Liza with their new dressage horse who was afraid of the horse trailer. Let me give Peter a call."

Peter confirmed that it was, in fact, Sofia, who had worked

with their horse, and they would strongly recommend using her. He told Jacob about how Sofia had trained the horse. He and Liza were especially happy that Sofia took her time with the training, so the horse was constantly relaxed and understood the task. Sofia trained their horse for a couple of days, before Peter took over the rope, and Sofia guided him in loading the horse. They hadn't had a problem since and the horse hauled just fine.

Jacob got Sofia's phone number and thanked Peter for his help.

Jacob repeated what Peter had said.

"I think Sofia may be the perfect trainer for Fly!" Nicholas exclaimed.

"What makes you say that?" Alice asked inquisitively, "just a gut feeling?"

"It's always a good idea to listen to your gut feeling and at least check out if it's right, don't you think?" Jacob asked, looking at Alice, who was drinking the last bit of her morning coffee.

With her mouth full, Alice nodded eagerly as she swallowed her coffee.

"Yes, Jacob, I agree. Would you call Sofia and tell her about Fly? See if she can help him?" she asked hopefully.

Jacob was happy to. Alice and Nicholas sat down close to Jacob, so they could hear what she said, because Jacob had put the call on speaker after dialing her number.

"This is Sofia," said a friendly voice on the telephone.

"Hi, my name is Jacob," he said.

"Hi, Jacob, how can I help you?" Sofia asked.

"I'm not even sure if you can help me. We have a three-year-old colt, which we have had for a couple of months. He came straight from the racetrack, where they had given up on him. They were about to send him to slaughter. My foster son fell in love with him, and they let us buy him. He seems to be a smart little guy. He doesn't seem mean, but he is generally very scared and shy. We have been working with him in the pasture, where he is with the other horses, but he won't let us near him. Do you think you can help us?"

"Do you know his background? Why did they give up on him?" Sofia asked thoughtfully.

Jacob told her everything they knew about Fly.

"It is our goal," he explained, "for Fly to get to know us, so we can handle him. You know – catch him, bring him into the stable, groom him, have him handled by the farrier and the vet. General horse handling. If we can accomplish even more with him, that would just be a bonus. But we will be happy if he can simply be handled."

"Okay, it sounds like I can help. I am sorry, but I am terrible at remembering names, what's his name again?" she asked.

"It's no problem. His name is Flying High, but we call him Fly." Jacob smiled through the phone.

"Okay, Jacob, I'd like to come see you. Then we can talk a little more about it, and I can evaluate Fly. That will also let you evaluate whether you want me for the job," she said.

Jacob looked first at Alice, who nodded, and then at Nicholas, who nodded eagerly and mouthed a "yes, yes."

"On our end, we agree that we would like that. What's your price?"

"Great! The initial evaluation is no charge. I charge $150 for each training session," she stated.

"That sounds reasonable. How many sessions do think it might take?" he asked.

"It's impossible to know before I meet Fly. But anywhere from one to six times. You will learn how to continue the work with him using the techniques I use, so you can keep up the training. You will get a training journal, and you can contact me along the way," she said.

"That sounds great. When can you come? We're retired and have lots of availability."

"Just a minute, let me find my calendar," she paused, "How about 4:00 pm next Wednesday?"

"That would be just fine. See you Wednesday at four.

We are really looking forward to it. By the way, we got your number from Peter and Liza, who were very happy with the work you did with their horse," Jacob said.

"Oh yes, I actually spoke with them the other day. We'll see you Wednesday. I look forward to meeting you all!" she said.

"Thank you so much, Sofia. Take care and see you soon!"

"Thank you! You too! Bye."

They both hung up.

"I can hardly wait," Nicholas said eagerly. "How many days until Wednesday?" he asked. He couldn't really remember the order of the days of the week.

"That's only three more days, Nico. Only three days until we know if Sofia will work with our little Fly," Alice answered kindly.

CHAPTER 26
Will Sofia train Fly?

On the beautiful sunny summer's day when Sofia was scheduled to come, there was peace and quiet in the horse pasture. Everyone was doing well.

Baby Aphrodite was starting to take an interest in the other horses in the string. She was curious and eager to learn. Alexandra was plenty busy keeping track of her, but the others had begun to help too. They'd entertain her, protect her from harm and make sure she stayed with the string. Scamp could get a little rough when he played with Aphrodite, but Fly was good at intervening and putting a bit of a damper on Scamp.

Aphrodite had also been introduced to Benji so they could continue their morning ritual of Benji running into the pasture to say hi to everyone without her getting scared.

Benji, Scamp, and Fly played their little game every day, and today, Aphrodite had stood there and looked at them with great interest. It probably wouldn't be long before she wanted to play too.

As usual at four o'clock in the afternoon, the horses had made it to the opposite side of the watering hole, which was opposite from the entrance to the pasture. When Sofia, Alice, Jacob, Nicholas, and Benji came down to the pasture, they couldn't see the horses, as they were behind the little knoll on the other side of the watering hole.

"Should we call them, or do you want to see them in their

usual routine?" Alice asked Sofia.

"I think it would be great to see them in their daily routine," Sofia answered.

"Well, then let's go in there. They are just on the other side at the knoll over there."

"Can I come too?" Nicholas asked.

Jacob said that he could come. And Benji could come too, if he wanted.

Together, they entered the pasture and passed the watering hole, and as they approached the top of the knoll, Jacob called Alexandra. He wanted to make sure that all the horses knew they were coming, so none of them would get scared; when Alexandra reacted to his call, the others would know that they were on their way.

Fly heard Jacob's voice before Alexandra reacted. As usual, he was on the alert more so than the others, and he heard every sound. But now he knew Jacob's voice, so he didn't get scared, although he was very observant. He stood with his head lifted and his ears pointed straight in the direction of the sound.

Now, he could hear steps in the grass as well. He noted that there were unfamiliar footsteps! It made him a bit uneasy, and he went over to Sir Howard to seek a little security from him.

Soon the humans appeared on the knoll. They stopped and looked at the horses.

Fly soon saw that there was a human he didn't know. So, he kept a sharp eye on it, and his heart rate increased.

When Sofia saw the horse string, she had no doubt which one was Fly because he was the only one aside from the foals that appeared tense. The other horses simply looked up, and once they had seen who was coming, they kept grazing. Sofia had heard the entire story about Fly and about Alice and Jacob training him.

"Can we sit in the grass and observe the horses for a while?"

she asked, "I would like to see how Fly does with the others."

"Sure!" Jacob answered.

When they had sat there for a little while, Fly started to relax and began grazing next to Sir Howard. Even so, he was keeping a good eye on them.

Suddenly they heard the sound of a motorcycle accelerating and driving off at a high speed. Fly startled and with a start, he spun around on his strong hind legs and took off at a full gallop away from the sound. When he stopped and turned to see if he was being pursued, Sofia could see that his nostrils were very dilated, his eyes were so big that you could see the white around the black pupil, and he was gasping for breath. She heard him huff loudly, which was allowing him to smell more efficiently.

Phew! Fly thought, *that was scary. I don't understand why the others don't get scared. Okay, I see that there is nothing here right now, but still, you never know if something might be coming to get us!*

When he had seen that there was no danger, he walked back to the others.

"Well, it is obvious that he has a strong reaction to things the others don't react to but at least he calmed down relatively quickly," Sofia said.

"Yes, though he has gotten better since his first day here," Alice said.

"Okay. Here's what I think," Sofia said, "first, I want to say that I would like to try to work with him. When I tune into him with my intuition, I get the feeling that he has a strong personality, he has a powerful sense of justice, that he is proud, intelligent, and quick to learn. Unfortunately, his experiences with humans have had a negative impact on him; his flight instinct is constantly active."

"Yes. It seems that your sense of him is the same as ours. We're hoping that his intelligence will aid him in learning to trust us," Jacob said.

"I won't give you false hope. I can't promise how far I can

get with him. After his first session I can give you a better idea," she said.

"Of course, Sofia," Jacob said. "Can you start today?"

"I would like to, if you have time. It might take a few hours. I need to set up a round pen, then we need to get Fly and one of the other horses in there."

"We have all the time you need!" Alice said. "We can help you with the round pen."

Nicholas was happy. He thought Sofia was fantastic, and he really thought she could help Fly.

CHAPTER 27
The First Session

Out in the pasture, they set up the round pen near the entrance. Sofia brought enough panels to create a large round pen. While they worked, she told them about her plan for that day's training.

"Normally I work with the horse alone in the round pen but since Fly is so scared of us, I will be using a different tactic. He clearly feels safe around the other horses so having a friend in there will make him feel better. Fly is convinced that humans and horses are a bad combination. He is clearly saying 'Thanks, but no thanks!'"

Nicholas laughed.

"I can tell you already know him, Sofia, what's your plan?" he asked.

Sofia explained, "I will use Howie to get Fly used to being in the round pen with me."

"Then you will keep both Howie and Fly loose in there?" Alice asked, a little worried.

"I was going to ask Jacob if he could lead Howie around in there. I'll guide him. What do you think, Jacob?" she asked, nodding toward him.

"Of course!" Jacob answered. "As long as I don't do anything that can damage Fly more than he has been already."

"You have a great sense of your horses; I don't think you will," Sofia reassured him. "My work is based on what the horse will go along with. If I can see that the horse is not up to the task, I'll back off a little until it kind of says 'yes' again. Once it's on board again and understands the task, I can take a small step forward. The most important thing is that the horse is always calm and positive about what I'm doing."

The horses had noticed that something was going on, so they had come over to follow the entire process.

Fly was there too, but he stayed at the back of the string. He was uneasy and his heart was pounding.

Everything new scared him.

"What is happening?" he asked the others.

"I don't know, little Fly. But it looks fascinating!" Sir Howard answered.

"How can you think that anything humans do is fascinating?" he asked, eyes worried.

Sir Howard laughed aloud at Fly's puzzled facial expression.

"We love our humans here at *Home of Love*, and they love us! So, when they do something, we know it's going to be fun and good for us. Let me ask you something: Have you experienced any of our humans doing anything unpleasant to you or any of us since you've been here?"

Fly looked at Sir Howard. He thought back at the past few months.

"No, I haven't. Now that I think about it, there have been lots of times when I have been worried and scared, but then they always stopped and walked away again. Hmm, maybe they aren't that bad after all," Fly said.

Fly watched as Alice, Jacob, and the new lady walked toward them. They were heading for Sir Howard.

With his head lifted high and with wide eyes and nostrils, Fly backed away from Sir Howard. Even though Howie was his support and his rock, and even though they had talked about it, he would rather not go too close to the humans.

Jacob had a rope in his hand. Fly saw it.

"Howie, run! They are bringing a snake!" he cried out in

fear.

Sir Howard looked at Jacob and turned to Fly.

"No, Fly. It's not a snake. It's a rope. It can't hurt us. You don't need to be afraid," he told him.

"Okay but what do they want?" he asked.

"I don't know, yet, but when they have a rope, it's usually because they want us to do something of some kind. Just stay with me, Fly, I will take care of you, there's no reason to be scared."

Fly calmed down a little. He fully trusted Sir Howard and he wanted his help and protection.

Fly decided that he would do as Sir Howard said. After all, he *could* always hightail it out of there if things got too dangerous.

When Jacob came over to Sir Howard, he reached out and petted his neck and his forehead, slipping a halter and lead rope over the gelding's head.

"Hey Howie, we have a little job for you today. Can you come to the round pen to help with Fly?" he said kindly, looking at the sweet horse.

Even thoug h Jacob knew Sir Howard didn't understand his words, he knew the tone of his voice reassured Sir Howard and invited him to follow. Jacob started toward the round pen.

Sir Howard looked at Fly, tossed back his head, and went with Jacob calmly. Sir Howard's little toss of the head told Fly that he should come along. Fly hesitated briefly, but then he took a deep breath and followed them. When they reached the round pen, Jacob and Sir Howard went in.

Fly stayed outside the entrance, a little uneasy. He stretched his neck as far as he could and sniffed with a loud snort. Jacob turned Sir Howard around, so he stood with his side to the entrance, and he, himself, stayed on the opposite side of Sir Howard.

Sir Howard stood completely calm, looking at Fly.

"Come on, Fly. It's fine!" he called. This made the difference in Fly choosing to join them. He passed the entrance in a quick jump and walked over to Sir Howard, but he remained alert.

His eyes and ears saw and heard everything around him. His beautiful chestnut body was tense and ready to flee. Sir Howard gave him a friendly little nudge to the shoulder.

"Just take it easy, Fly. Nothing bad will happen to us."

Fly relaxed a little again, but he was still alert to everything. Sofia walked into the round pen and closed the gate.

"Will you walk Howie around along the fence?" she asked, "Then I will see how Fly reacts to my being here in the middle."

"Of course," Jacob answered as he calmly began walking Sir Howard around the ring.

Fly followed, half trotting and half plodding. His head and tail were lifted high, and he emptied his stomach for content so he was ready to run, should it become necessary.

With calm eyes, a relaxed body, and her side facing them, Sofia studied all three of them. She was careful not to look Fly straight in the eye.

In horse language, eye contact is akin to a scolding. Direct eye contact for an extended period means that you are telling it to go away. Also, if you are facing the horse, the eye contact is emphasized; the horse truly believes that you want it to go far away and as fast as possible. In the case of Fly, it was the last thing they wanted him to think.

When they had walked around the pen about eight times, Sofia noticed that Fly was beginning to relax some. His neck, head and tail were lowered a bit. These were some of the signs she waited for to tell her that Fly was getting calmer. She took a step forward, lifted her right arm, and asked Jacob to stop and go the other way. A horse's sight is predominantly peripheral. If they don't see things with both eyes, they don't interpret it properly. Everything is new for them twice. Because of this, it's important to do everything from both sides of the horse if you want them to understand it completely.

Fly reacted as Sofia had expected when they walked the other way. Once again, he lifted his tail uneasily. This was completely normal, so Sofia simply continued to observe him. At the same time, she was aware that Sir Howard was half-asleep, following Jacob around the round pen calmly.

It didn't take long before she saw the expression in Fly's eyes become calmer and he lowered his neck and tail again.

This time a little lower.

Again, she took a step forward and lifted her left arm, after which she asked Jacob to stop and go the other way.

I wonder what this is all about, Fly thought when they had turned around for the second time. *It really isn't as bad as I thought it would be. That lady didn't seem dangerous at all, and her body language told me what to do.*

Sofia saw that one of Fly's ears was starting to turn toward her all the time, his neck and throat were more relaxed, and his tail was close to being in a normal position.

The many signs of Fly relaxing made her very happy, and the fact that his ear was tuned to her meant that he understood that she wanted something from him. Finally came the last signal Sofia was waiting for. Fly licked and chewed.

The second she saw that, she took another step forward, but this time she turned around and stood with her back to Fly. She stood completely still with her shoulders low and a calm posture. She asked Jacob to come in and stand next to her along with Sir Howard.

Sofia asked Alice to tell her what Fly was doing from outside the round pen.

"He stopped at the fence when Jacob and Howie went over to you," she answered. "Now, he is standing still and looking away from you. Now he is looking at you, he is tossing his head back a little. Now looking away. Now looking at you again and turning toward you. Now he is tossing back his head again."

Alice was so surprised by Fly's reaction that her voice broke from emotion, and she almost couldn't continue because of the lump in her throat. She swallowed hard. "Awww … he is going in by you!! He is stopping, but he is standing right behind you!"

A big burden was lifted from Alice's heart, and she was overcome with joy. She let out a little sob. This was much better than she had dared hope for.

Nicholas didn't even realize it, but tears of joy were rolling down his cheeks because Fly had chosen to go in by Sofia *completely voluntarily.*

Before Fly made the choice to go in with Sofia and the others, he had debated it quite a bit. He stopped and looked in at the others.

Why are they going in there? Should I run away? He looked out to the pasture, but there was a fence between the pasture and himself. He looked at the others again, and particularly at Sofia.

She invited me, the way we do it with each other when we have been scolded and we are being told that it's okay, and we can return to the string. But let me just wait and see if she really means it!

He waited to see if Sofia would stay there, or if she would do something else.

Okay! It appears she means it and Howie is there too.

When he had made the decision to trust that he had interpreted Sofia's body language and signals correctly, he tossed his head back to show that he knew what he was doing. Then he went in and placed himself near Sofia's shoulder like he would have done if she were a horse who had invited him to come over.

While Sofia deliberately took deep, calm breaths, she carefully reached her hand back toward Fly's muzzle, as she took a slow step backwards, so she was standing next to Fly's head.

Howie was standing on the other side of Fly, and Jacob on the outside of Howie.

Sofia didn't say anything. She looked at Fly's face, but without looking into his eyes. By allowing Fly to see her eyes and their expression, he could decide for himself whether he liked what he saw. He could also sniff her hand. If he didn't like the scent, he could simply walk away.

Sofia gave Fly time to decide.

This is not too bad! In fact, it feels pretty good being here with Sofia.

Fly let out a faint sigh, lowered his head, telling Sofia that he had accepted being with her.

Sofia carefully placed her hand in the middle of Fly's shoulder.

She took a deep breath, stood completely still, and enjoyed the unique moment when Fly had said "yes, please" to being her friend.

These moments were the most priceless in her work with the horses, and she would do anything to protect this friendship. It was important that she didn't break the trust Fly had just shown her.

All friendships are fragile, but a friendship with a damaged horse that has been subjected to human cruelty can be damaged again with a single wrong action. In a moment, the horse can get a thought or feeling like *Told you so! It was dangerous! Let me get out of here!*

Sofia decided to wrap up the first session on this note. She lowered her hand from Fly's shoulder, turned her head, and walked away from Fly.

"Fly has done a perfect join-up by coming in by me. Most times, I keep working with the horse doing follow-up, touching, lifting hooves, etc. But in Fly's severe case, I won't give him any more today. I worry about damaging any of what we achieved today. Is that okay with you?" she asked.

"Oh, my goodness, yes!" Alice exclaimed from outside the

round pen. "What you achieved with Fly is simply amazing, and much more than I thought possible in such a short time!"

"I agree!" Jacob chimed in from the other side of Sir Howard.

"You are so amazing!" Nicholas cheered. His happy outburst made the others laugh, lightening the seriousness of the session.

Laughing, Sofia went over and opened the gate to the round pen so Jacob, Sir Howard, and Fly could go out to the other horses. The string had lost interest along the way, and now stood grazing further out in the pasture.

"Thank you so much for your help, Howie! It wouldn't have been the same without help from you, buddy!" Jacob took his halter off and petted Sir Howard on his favorite spot under his forelock.

When Sofia closed the gate to the round pen behind them, she asked if they wanted her to come back for another session with Fly.

"We don't even need to discuss it! There's no doubt that you're the best trainer for Fly," Alice and Jacob said together.

"Thank you," Sofia said warmly. "Is it okay to leave the round pen up?"

"Of course," Jacob answered. "It's not in the way of anything here."

Nicholas was dying to get Sofia to explain more about what happened when she turned to invite Fly to join her.

"I'm sorry, but it was crazy exciting when you were waiting to see if Fly would come in to join you. Will you tell me more about it?"

Sofia gave Nicholas' arm a friendly squeeze.

"You are so sweet, Nicholas, and I love that you like the work. Let me tell you…"

"I'm sorry to interrupt you, Sofia, but how about we go up and get something to eat; you can tell us about it while I cook?" Alice asked. The others noticed suddenly how hungry they had become, so everyone thought that was a great idea.

CHAPTER 28
When the Horse Chooses to Join Up

Sofia, Nicholas, and Jacob were sitting around the table in the cozy kitchen, while Alice cooked supper. Benji was lying with his head on his front paws at Jacob's feet dozing but still with an eye on his humans.

Dusk fell softly and slowly over the little farm, *Home of Love*, and all its inhabitants. The cats were waking, ready to live their night life in the dark hunting for prey. Some of the hens had climbed into their nests, and others were finding their places on the roost for the night. The horses had gone down to the watering hole to quench their thirst before taking turns sleeping, resting, and keeping watch.

Sofia told them more about the work she had done with Fly today.

"As you may remember, I told you about the little bit of trust Fly showed me by stopping at the fence and looking at me, and this is why I needed Alice to tell me what he was doing."

The others nodded.

"As I said, I do things differently than most trainers. It's important to evaluate each horse to see what they need and where their limits are. You did a good job with him before I came, he's had time to become calmer," she paused, not wanting to offend them. She thought about it.

"My experience and sense of Fly is that he is terribly damaged, and it is a big job to get him to want to be with us – with humans in general," she continued, "As you told me, he was completely green when he came to the racetrack; nobody taught him how to be with humans. On the contrary, every time they wanted something from him, his experience was nothing but anxious and painful," she said sadly.

"Horses are prey animals; they have an amazing memory. It helps them stay alive by avoiding things that are dangerous, for instance. Even though horses have been living with humans for thousands of years, their ancient instincts are still relevant; they live for the survival of the species.

"Horses, like all prey animals, have three basic instincts: food, herd, and flight instincts. This means that they need food and water. They need other horses for protection against enemies, so they don't get killed and devoured. They also need other horses so they can breed and ensure the survival of the species."

Nicholas had gotten up while Sofia was talking, but he hung on to her every word while he set the table and filled the water pitcher. That was his job every evening, and after supper all three of them helped each other clear the table and do the dishes. It was cozy, doing things together, and they would talk about their day.

"In Fly's case, both his flight instinct and his herd instinct had been under intense pressure. There was nowhere to flee, and there was nobody to help and protect him when he was at the racetrack. He remembers that clearly, and he will remember it for the rest of his life. To him, humans equal pain and bad, incomprehensible experiences.

"When horses communicate with each other or with other animals and humans, they mainly use their bodies. They only use sounds a little bit. If they are too loud, it is easier for their enemies to find them. We humans also use body language with each other, but we do it more subconsciously. Horses can't learn to use our body language, but we can learn to use theirs."

"I would love to learn a lot more about body language!" Nicholas said with such sincerity and eagerness in his voice, that the others laughed good-naturedly.

"Sweet Nico," Jacob said, "you're so passionate about horses with all your heart. You'll have the opportunity to learn much more. Maybe Sofia can come teach us!" Jacob looked at Sofia. "Do you give lessons in horsemanship?"

"Yes, I do! I'd be happy to do some here with you!" Sofia exclaimed.

"Whoo-hoo!" Nicholas cheered, clapping his hands with a huge smile. Sofia laughed in amusement.

"When I come here to work with Fly, you'll also learn a lot. The work with him won't be finished until at least one of you can go into the field, put a halter on him, and bring him into to the stable. Afterwards, we can arrange some lessons at your house," Sofia said smiling. The others nodded.

"But back to Fly and what happened in the round pen today," she continued. "His body language told me he realized I understood him.

"First, he relaxed in the neck more and more, lowering his head a little, he wasn't in such a high state of alert. You could say that he lowered his defenses a little. Later, as he becomes familiar with us, he'll lower his head completely, until his muzzle is near the ground when he trots or gallops.

"Next, he turned one ear toward me, and it was practically glued in my direction. That showed that he was listening to me.

"Finally, he licked his lips, or at least he stuck his tongue out a couple of times with a bit of a munching motion. That sign means that he understands me, and that he is willing to eat in my presence; that he doesn't consider me an enemy. Does that make sense?" she asked, looking at the others. All three of them nodded eagerly.

"It makes perfect sense," Alice answered. "Even though I might have known a little bit about these things, I have never had it explained so simply and clearly. You sure have taught me a lot of new, exciting things today! What about you, Jacob?" she asked, turning toward her husband.

"I agree wholeheartedly, Alice. I'm fascinated with what you have told us, Sofia. Question: why did you choose to turn around and invite fly to join you at that very moment? Why was the timing right? And why couldn't you look at him afterwards?"

"Thank you so much for your kind words." Sofia looked down at the table shyly looking at her plate with little, pale blue flowers around the edge.

"That was exactly what I wanted to tell you, but once I get started, I get so excited that I start rambling about all kinds of other things.

"Well, the right time to invite the horse to join up is knowing how to recognize when the horse is ready; that it got the message. The more sensitive a horse is, the more precisely I need to react, with Fly it is at the very moment he says 'now, I understand'.

"If I react too late, the horse can think or feel that I don't understand it. It may decide that I don't have the ability or skill for it to trust me. It won't believe that I can benefit from it.

"It's like when you say 'yes' to another person, but the other person asks again, and you say yes again. If the person asks you again, you will probably start to wonder if you understood the question, or whether the person heard or understood your answer.

"If the horse isn't sure about me, then I can't win its trust. Without trust, it's impossible to get somebody like Fly to want to be with us. After all, he knows that we belong to his enemies, the hunters, and that he is the prey.

"So, when Fly licked and chewed, he was showing that he was willing to eat in my presence. When the horse is willing to do that, it shows that it feels safe. It can't see very far when its head is down grazing, making it slower to flee. This makes it more at risk of being eaten by predators. By turning away at the very second, he was licking and chomping, I showed him that I understood his message," she said.

The others nodded thoughtfully.

"Next, he hesitated for a little bit before choosing to come. He was evaluating whether I understood him completely. If I had looked at him with my 'predator eyes', he might have thought that I was trying to trick him or lure him over to me, so I could eat him. There were quite a few things for him to consider within a short time.

"Horses are quick to make decisions and take stock of their surroundings, but they need us to give them time. If we give them a command, we give them time to think about it, then follow the command. Just like we humans do with each other and with our other animals. Does that make sense?" she asked. She looked from one to the next, and they all expressed that it made very good sense.

"Time to eat!" Alice said, "I bet you are starving. I am, anyway!"

Benji woke up from his slumber when he heard the word 'eat'. Alice called him as she placed his food bowl on the floor and he jumped up like a rocket; as always, he was ravenous as well.

CHAPTER 29
The Big Breakthrough

"What do you expect will happen with Fly today?" Nicholas asked with anticipation. He and Sofia were making their way down to the pasture.

"It is only the second day, so I don't expect a whole lot from him today. We will start the training exactly like we started it yesterday. Meaning Jacob and Sir Howard are with us in the round pen, walking along the fence according to my direction. I will do the join-up with Fly again. The goal for today is for him to do a follow-up with me afterwards."

"What's a follow-up?" Nicholas asked.

Alice and Jacob were familiar with expression and generally knew what it was, but they were also excited to hear Sofia's explanation.

"Like join-up, follow-up is a horse training expression. In this work, join-up means that the horse comes over to me. Follow-up means that it follows me without using a rope or other equipment, but rather of its own free will."

"Wow, that will be exciting!" Nicholas said.

"Nico, you actually did follow-up with him when he followed you up into the truck at the racetrack!" she said with a smile.

Jacob had placed his hand amicably on Nicholas' shoulder and gave it a little squeeze. Nicholas looked wide-eyed at Jacob, his mouth falling open as he tried to remember that day at the racetrack.

"Wow! That was a follow-up?" he exclaimed.

Sofia opened her eyes wide and nodded.

"Did he follow you up into the truck without a lead rope or anything?" she asked, her voice heavy with respect.

"Yes," Nicholas answered. "He did!"

"Well Nico, I've got to hand it to you, that was nothing less than fantastic! You've got quite the flair for working with horses."

Nicholas blushed at her praise, but his eyes sparkled with pride. Jacob gave Nicholas' shoulder another loving squeeze.

"Yes, we have a very talented young man here. We're hoping Fly and Nico will have a great relationship and be able to work together."

"Well, let's get started, so we can get a step closer to that goal," Sofia said. She gave Nicholas an encouraging smile.

Sofia had guided Jacob to lead Sir Howard around the round pen; first one way, and then the other way, and back the first way again. She once again invited Fly to come in with them by doing a join-up. Fly was much more relaxed in the round pen today. He showed the three signals more clearly and significantly faster. He was a sensitive but smart horse. He remembered the prior day's work clearly, and he felt safe about everything progressing in the exact same way.

When Sofia invited him to join up, he spent just a second evaluating whether he wanted to accept the invitation.

"He is looking at you. He is going to join you. He's standing at your shoulder!" Alice knew her job and provided Sofia with the necessary information, so she didn't have to look back at Fly.

Sofia turned halfway and took a couple of steps back, so she was standing next to Fly's head.

This is actually nice! Fly thought. He relaxed and allowed Sofia to touch his shoulder. He noticed that she barely touched him before removing her hand again while she turned her body and eyes away from him. It made him look at her with slight puzzlement, but he wasn't scared.

I wonder what you're doing now? he thought.

Sofia repeated the exercise of putting her hand on his shoulder, removing it again, and turning away from him two more times.

Fly stood completely still, waiting.

Okay, when she moves away like that without me doing anything at all, at least she isn't trying to eat me. And it didn't hurt either!

He turned his head toward Sofia to show her that he accepted her and what she was doing.

Sofia placed her hand on his back. Three times, she repeated the whole exercise of removing her hand before turning her body and averting her gaze.

Fly followed her with his eyes and stood completely still. It was clear to him that nothing unpleasant was happening when he stood completely still.

While Sofia repeated the same exercise on different areas of Fly's body, she told the others what was happening.

"It turns out that horses react very well when you repeat new things with them three times in a row. This, however, must be three times of the horse reacting correctly. If it isn't standing still, or if it does the exercise wrong the third time, then we must start over and repeat it until it does it right three times in a row.

"It's all about the fact that when we do a new exercise with the horse, then it doesn't know what we expect or what it should do. So, the first time we give a command, it simply does what it thinks we want – it takes a guess.

"The second time we give the command, it starts to think about what's happening. If it gets confused or doesn't understand the command, it may react differently from the first time.

"If it does it correctly the second and third times, then it is doing the exercise deliberately, meaning it knows what it's doing, and it knows that when we give it this command, we are looking for this reaction," she explained.

Sofia placed her hand on Fly's neck, and he tossed his head into the air with a start, his black mane and forelock billowing around him, and he quickly took a step away from Sofia.

No, no, that's too dangerous! Not my head!

"This is a good example of him saying 'no, thank you!'" Sofia explained.

"He is showing me that I am progressing too fast, and that he's not up to it. Now, it's my job to show him that I didn't mean any harm, which is why I take a step back and I repeat one of the exercises from when he still felt safe and wasn't moving. Back to when he was still saying 'yes, please'."

Sofia placed her hand on his shoulder three times.

Fly stood still. This was something he recognized, and he knew from before that it wasn't dangerous.

The fourth time, Sofia placed her hand on him an inch or two closer to his neck.

Well, okay. That's probably okay too! It's not too different from before! Fly thought, standing still while Sofia placed her hand in the exact same spot two more times.

This way, she worked inch by inch, further and further up Fly's neck toward his head.

Just once, he took a step away again. Sofia moved her hand back to the previous place.

After that, Fly allowed her to continue.

Finally, Sofia could place her hand on Fly's jaw, and even on the bridge of his nose.

Now, Fly was standing with his head down, resting one hind leg. He was completely relaxed and feeling secure.

"I know it took some time to get this far," Sofia said, "but the beginning is especially important. This is where we build trust. If I proceed too quickly without checking if Fly is completely onboard and saying yes to each exercise, I can lose it all, and then we must start over."

The others had been following her with fascination.

"It has been so interesting, but I don't think it has taken all that long at all," Jacob said.

The others agreed. They had been following along from the other side of the round pen and watched closely.

Uh-oh! Fly thought, becoming slightly more alert.

He became slightly uneasy when Sofia started to walk slowly in front of him and to his other side. First, she was now standing between him and Sir Howard, and secondly, he didn't know what was about to happen. The situation was different!

Sofia was now standing to Fly's right side. She placed her hand on his shoulder. She repeated the entire procedure that she had been through on his left side.

First, by placing her hand on his shoulder, then his back, and then other areas of his body.

She finished by placing her hand on his neck several times, all the way up to his head, on his jaw, and finally on the bridge of his nose.

It felt a little less safe for Fly when she did it on his right side.

He wasn't at all used to humans doing anything on that side, and so for him, it was completely unfamiliar. However, he had developed trust in Sofia, that helped him understand it was okay though he preferred to have her on his left side.

"Most horses are not used to being handled from the right side. I think we need to be better at doing everything from both sides. It isn't harder for the horse to learn. It's probably laziness on our part that we don't get them used to it, perhaps because we learned that way from the beginning, and because most of us are right-handed, so it is easier to do most things from the left side of the horse," Sofia chuckled.

"By doing everything from both sides, we are training ourselves to be better, stronger, and more flexible in our left side. In fact, as riders and trainers, it's important we are as symmetrical as possible."

Sofia returned to Fly's right side.

The next exercise served to show Fly that she wouldn't attack him in places where his natural enemies would normally attack him.

She placed her hand on his throat and let it slide slowly toward his chest.

Fly lifted his head slightly and was very aware of her movements, but he stood still.

Sofia placed her hand on his mane and let it slide down his back to his hind quarters.

She moved her hand behind his foreleg and let her hand slide along his belly. She made sure to keep a light, but still firm, touch to avoid tickling him.

Fly relaxed more and more in the process. He understood that she wasn't about to eat him, because she would have lodged a bite in one of the vulnerable places where she had touched him.

Sofia repeated everything on his left side.

"The last exercise before I do follow-up is that I lift his leg. Not high, but just enough to get his hoof off the ground," she said.

"But he's not used to that!" Alice exclaimed with alarm. "What if he kicks you?"

"Well, I don't do this exercise until the horse is wearing a halter with a rope. I'm only going to lift his front hooves, so I avoid being kicked."

"What's the purpose of that?" Jacob asked.

"When the horse lifts one hoof and lets us hold it, it's showing us a huge amount of trust. The horse believes that we control that one leg, and consequently we're robbing it of the opportunity to flee if that should become necessary or something it wants to do."

"Wow!" Nicholas exclaimed. "I didn't know that, but couldn't it just pull back on the leg to flee?"

"Yes, it can. But for some reason the horse doesn't see it that way," Sofia explained.

She was now standing close to Fly's shoulder with her back to his head. She let her hand slide down his foreleg.

When her hand was just above the hoof, she leaned in on him slightly to change his center of gravity a little.

Fly felt the pressure, shifted his weight slightly to his right foreleg and lifted the left hoof an inch or two from the ground. Sofia let go of the hoof, straightened up, took a step back and turned away from Fly. This told him that it was exactly what she was asking, and that she removed the pressure.

She repeated it two more times and Fly willingly lifted his hoof both times.

Alice, Jacob, and Nicholas had waited with bated breath, while Sofia had lifted the hoof. They breathed a sigh of relief after Sofia had let go of the hoof for the third time and had stepped away from Fly.

"You're so good, Sofia!" Jacob exclaimed spontaneously.

"I hadn't thought it possible. Not in my wildest imagination!" Alice said with admiration.

"Once the horse has done such a great join-up as Fly did, it is usually just a question of doing the rest in the right way," Sofia explained as she moved calmly to Fly's other side.

This time, he was completely calm, even though she was standing between him Sir Howard.

Once Fly had lifted his left front hoof the first time, he became a little uneasy anyway.

Uh…maybe this isn't quite okay? He started to move away.

Gently, Sofia placed a hand on his shoulder and followed him.

After a few steps, Fly stopped again and stood still. That very second, Sofia let go of his shoulder, took a step back and turned away from him – thus relieving him of all the pressure.

She definitely isn't trying to eat me, or else she wouldn't have walked away when I stopped!

Fly looked at Sofia, licked his lips, and chomped. Sofia saw his reaction and knew that he had now understood that she wasn't going to hurt him.

Once again, she got ready to lift his right front hoof. This time, Fly stood still when she let it go again, and he let her lift it two more times.

Now, Sofia turned around and stood by Fly's head. She addressed Fly's family.

"This was a good example of the horse doing what I ask even though he doesn't understand the task or feels uneasy about it. When Fly walked away after I lifted the hoof the first time, I followed him, and I walked away from him when he *stopped* and stood still. By following him, I pressured him a little, and when he stopped, the pressure was removed. This is called "press and release." Press when the horse is doing the wrong thing, and release when it does the right thing. When we use that system, most horses learn quickly what we want them to do. We do it in small steps, so they are always close to saying yes rather than just running away screaming.

We know press and release from riding. When riding, we push with our legs to get the horse to move forward. That's pressing. We stop pressing when it goes forward. That's release. If we get better at using it when we are dealing with the horse from the ground, it will understand us much better," Sofia explained.

Alice and Jacob looked at each other and nodded; it made perfect sense.

"Now, I'll start doing a follow-up with him," Sofia said. She had gone over to Fly's left side, where he felt most comfortable with her.

She stood slightly behind his head and took a step forward and to the right, so she pressured him a little. She continued forward in a calm, gliding movement with firm steps.

Fly reacted to her movement by turning his head a little to the right. That way he avoided having her touch him with her shoulder.

He had gotten a little out of balance, so he took a step forward and to the side. This set him in motion, so he continued to walk.

I know this! This is also what we do when we ask each other to come along.

Sofia walked in a little circle to the right. Then she made a quick and clear stop, which made Fly stop as well.

Sofia couldn't help smiling with satisfaction over Fly's perfect reaction. He was just so sweet and wonderful, and he was doing all the right things. She praised him with a friendly voice and petted his neck before repeating everything one more time.

When Fly had gone with her three times to the right, she didn't stop, but rather continued in a little circle to the left. Fly followed her and stopped when she stopped.

This is a fun game, he thought.

Nicholas reached for Alice's hand, the two emotional about what they were seeing between Fly and Sofia. Nicholas gave her hand a little squeeze.

"Okay!" Sofia said, when she stopped for the last time, "his reaction is just perfect. Better than most others I had worked with. I think he may be ready with a rope and maybe a halter today."

She looked around and saw that there was a halter and a rope lying just outside the round pen. When she went to get it, Fly followed. Jacob looked on, speechless.

"Whoa, look! He's following you! It's just *incredible!*" he exclaimed in surprise.

Sofia turned her head a little and saw Fly following her over to the fence. *Now,* she was sure she could proceed with the next exercise.

CHAPTER 30

Did that really happen?

Fly had accepted Sofia, and for the first time in his life, he felt comfortable being with a human. He trusted her and felt understood.

He saw that she started to walk.

I'd better go with her. It feels nice and safe being with her; what is she doing?

He looked at Sofia inquisitively when she bent over and grabbed the rope and the halter lying outside the fence. She held it close to her body.

He furrowed his brow a little.

Hmmm, I don't know if I like that – but okay, let me see what's going to happen.

He followed Sofia to the middle of the round pen and stopped when she stopped. He watched as she placed the halter on the ground. Now, she was only holding the rope in her hand, bundled.

Fly lifted his head a little when she held the rope up to his muzzle. When he saw that she didn't do anything else, he lowered his head and sniffed her hand. He could smell the rope as well, and it smelled like Alexandra.

Sofia moved her hand back after Fly had sniffed it. She reached it out again.

Fly didn't lift his head this time, instead he immediately stuck his muzzle up to the hand. He knew this game now: if he stood still, the pressure went away.

Sofia repeated the exercise two more times without Fly moving his head. She went down to Fly's left shoulder, placing the hand that held the rope on his shoulder. She made sure the rope didn't touch him.

Fly got a little insecure. He pulled back his shoulder with a little jerk and looked at Sofia.

Sofia left her hand on his shoulder, until Fly was completely relaxed again.

When he started chomping, she removed her hand and her gaze and turned away from him a little. When she put the hand back a second time, he was completely calm and didn't react at all.

The third and fourth times, he almost looked like he was bored, which made Sofia smile. This was exactly what she was trying to accomplish – that he wouldn't care what she did.

The training continued in the same way all over his body, and, of course, on the other side as well.

It was time to show Fly more of the rope in Sofia's hand. Again, Sofia started by letting Fly sniff it. She held a little bit of the rope between her hands.

Fly reached out his muzzle and sniffed the rope. *It smells like Alexandra. That's too funny!* Both because it smelled like Alexandra, and because Sofia was holding the rope the way she did, he didn't associate it with a snake, like he had done previously.

Slowly, Sofia showed Fly more and more of the rope.

He felt completely safe about it. He was even curious enough to grab it with his teeth and pull on it a little and taste it before letting go again. He tossed his head up and down several times while alternately yawning loudly and licking his lips.

Alice, Nicholas, and Jacob laughed, and it eased the tension they had felt since Sofia started working with the rope.

It didn't taste as good as I thought!

Fly's forelock flapped around his ears when he tossed his

head.

Sofia moved on to his shoulder where she repeated the same exercises as before, but now the rope was touching Fly when she put her hand on him.

Fly stood completely calm and relaxed, letting Sofia work with the rope on his body on both the left side and the right. He didn't even react when she placed a little bit of the rope over his back and took it back again. He also allowed her to reach one arm under his neck and pet him on the other side of the neck.

"Now, I'm going to try it with the halter," she said. Fly watched as she put down the rope and picked up the halter. He kept an eye on what she was doing, but otherwise he stood completely still, resting on one hind leg.

"Nico, do you see how he is resting on one leg?" Alice whispered to Nicholas.

"Yes, he is so calm! You would think it was a completely different horse, rather than our scared little Fly," he whispered back.

Alice nodded.

Sofia presented the halter to Fly in the exact same way she had done with the rope.

While she was working, she suddenly had the familiar feeling that everything was harmonious.

Carefully, but without hesitation, she pulled the nose strap over his muzzle and positioned it on the bridge of his nose.

Carefully, she removed it again.

She repeated this three times, and every time it was as though fly shrugged his shoulders and didn't care – at least he didn't react to it.

The fourth time, she placed the neck strap across his neck and removed it again.

The fourth time, she buckled it, so Fly was now wearing the halter.

She lowered her arms, took a little step away from him and stood completely still.

Fly turned his head and looked at her.

He felt the halter moving on his head, and he froze and held his breath. In a flash, he saw an image in his head from the pasture, where he was lying on the ground with several of the humans on top of him as they forced the halter onto his head. *No, no, no,* he thought with a tinge of desperation, before he fortunately realized where he was, and that he was with everyone he trusted and knew.

He turned his head and looked at Sir Howard, having nearly forgotten that he was there with him.

"Howie! You were right. It's not all that bad!"

Sir Howard breathed a sigh of relief and laughed out loud. "

"You're so cool, Fly! I'm so proud of you, buddy, so proud!" His big body was shaking with laughter.

Fly laughed too, and he appreciated Sir Howard's praise.

Once Sofia saw that Fly had calmed down and had accepted the halter, she stepped up to him again and took it off. Nicholas' eyes opened wide.

"Aw! Why is she taking it off again?!" he asked, dismayed. Before Jacob or Alice had time to answer him, Sofia had already put the halter back on Fly again. Nicholas let out a sigh of relief.

"Oh, I should have known that she would do it again three times," he laughed.

And that's exactly what she did.

When she had put it on him for the third time, she asked Alice to come join them.

"Me?" Alice asked surprised, pointing back at herself.

"Yes. Fly is ready for you to take over."

Sofia stood with one hand on Fly's neck to show him that she was still focusing on him, even though she was addressing Alice.

Alice was a little nervous as she entered the round pen. Sofia calmed her down by explaining that she should just take slow, deep breaths and approach facing them with her side.

Alice did as she said, and once she was standing next to

Sofia and Fly, she was calm and ready.

"Put your hand next to mine…Now, let it slide up his neck … lift your other hand up to the halter … unbuckle the neck strap … slowly, let the halter slide off him … take a step back and turn your back to him … turn back around and walk over to him … put the halter back on …"

Sofia calmly guided Alice in slipping the halter on and off of Fly's head. Her voice broke a little as she praised Alice with tears in her eyes.

"You are so good at this, Alice! That is *precisely* the way to do it," she said quietly.

A tear rolled down her cheek and she cleared her throat, petting Fly on the shoulder.

"And *you* are so good, Fly!" she praised.

Fly was now fully aware that it was Alice and not Sofia who took off the halter and put it back on. The way everything was happening made him feel completely safe about it. When Alice took off the halter and put it on again two more times, he helped her by sticking his muzzle into the halter before she had time to lift it up to him.

"Wow!" Jacob's voice was full of admiration. "That's crazy … if I hadn't seen it with my own eyes, I wouldn't have believed it had happened! Alice … Sofia, it's a miracle!"

"It *is* a miracle!" Nicholas repeated. "It's like an adventure … one of the ones that have a happy ending."

They all laughed in agreement. Fly tossed back his head.

"Fly agrees with you too," Alice said, putting a loving, gentle hand on Fly's neck. "I love you, little Fly, and we'll figure everything out together, I promise. We will help you!"

Fly didn't understand a word of what Alice was saying, but the kindness in her tone, her relaxed posture, and breathing, along with the gentle touch to his neck, told him that it was a nice and safe place to be right now.

I never thought I would be so close to humans, but it's really very nice. They are not so dangerous after all … at least not these humans.

Fly hadn't been so happy since he was with his mom and all the others in the big summer pasture where he was born.

CHAPTER 31
But now what, and will it work in the future?

Later that day, Sofia and the little family gathered in the kitchen.

"If you can take notes and make a few videos of your training, then I can follow how it's going. That way I can help you if there are problems," she said to them.

Alice, Jacob, and Nicholas followed the instructions Sofia gave them with great interest. Benji was lying in his dog bed in the kitchen, and the others were sitting around the table. They had just finished eating the delicious lunch Alice and Jacob had prepared.

"Is this the last day you'll be here?" Nicholas asked with a sad look on his face.

"No, Nico," Sofia smiled. "At the very least, I will be here for the next four days. We will make a training schedule that we will follow while I'm here, and which you will continue to work on afterwards."

Nicholas breathed a sigh of relief, happy that Sofia would be back as he had grown very fond of her. He was learning so much.

"Tomorrow we'll start with you, Alice, being in the round pen along with Jacob, Howie and myself. I will walk behind you, while you do a join-up and a follow-up with Fly. After the follow-up I want you to take the halter off and put it back on three times.

"After that, I'll continue to train with him on the next step.

I am going to attach the rope to the halter and teach him to be led. Hopefully, it will go just as well as the rest has gone until now. We'll finish up with you working with him on the rope as well. How does that sound?" Sofia asked. She paused and gave the others an inquiring look.

"What if I can't do the join-up or follow-up?" Alice asked a little nervously.

"If you have a problem, I can take over right away, since I'm right behind you all the time. You don't need to worry."

Alice drew a breath of relief. Jacob looked at Sofia.

"How many days do we need to have Howie with us in the round pen?" he asked.

"I don't expect to need him for more than another two days. After those two days, Alice can do all the work with Fly by herself in the round pen," Sofia said.

"On day three, Alice will do all the same work in the round pen without you, Jacob or Howie. After that, we will go outside the pen with Fly, asking Howie again to lead the way. We will go around the pasture with them for a while before letting them go."

Sofia pointed to the computer screen as she explained her plan to them.

"The next day, we'll do the same thing. If leading them around the pasture goes well, we'll go up to the stable and back again with both horses.

"We are going to take a day off on day five. You will likely find that Fly has developed a whole lot when we work with him after his day off. Like us, the animals need to recover and relax, both in mind and body.

"The sixth day will probably be the last one working in the round pen. If everything goes as I expect, we will pull them into the stable and spend some quality time with them there. It would be great if you have some treats for them that they can eat during that time."

"We have lots of apples and carrots from the garden," Nicholas said. "I'll make sure we have some for them!"

"Perfect, Nico!" Sofia said, giving him a friendly smile. She had grown fond of all three of them, but especially of Nicholas. He had a heart of gold.

"From here, you will work independently, following the training journal. And, as I mentioned, I'm still with you online. What do you think?" Sofia made a sweeping gesture with both hands and looked at them.

"Sounds good but what if Fly regresses?" Jacob asked worried.

"That's a great question, Jacob, and it was my next point. You can read here …" Sofia indicated on the computer where it was written. "Here, I wrote a little about what you can do if you have problems. For instance, if he won't go with you and Howie, if he gets scared of something and tries to run away, if he walks away from you when you go to get him from the pasture, things like that. Does that make sense?"

Alice read a little of the text, nodding.

"What an impressive and thorough work plan you have made, Sofia!" she said.

"Thank you, Alice. When you share the journal and videos with me, I can help you along the way. If you have problems that are too difficult, I'll just come back."

"Is it good enough if Nico records the videos on his cell phone?" Jacob asked.

"That's perfect," she answered. "It doesn't have to be fancy, just so I can see what's going on."

Sofia showed them that the work plan covered the next four weeks.

"When we are done with the training, does that mean Fly is cured?" Nicholas asked.

Sofia looked at him, choosing her words carefully.

"I have to say that I can't guarantee that he is healed. As with humans, horses remember their experiences for the rest of their lives, specifically, the bad ones. By showing them things in a different way, we may be able to get them to accept it while feeling safe and having trust. However, if something happens that makes them remember their old bad experiences, they can regress.

"There was once another driver that hit me. My car was badly damaged, and I was in the hospital with a broken leg, two teeth knocked out, and a concussion. Now, every time I drive in that same spot or if I am in a similar situation, I feel anxious and scared that it might happen again, even though I know that it probably won't. The experience stays in my body and my memory, and then I react automatically when something happens that looks like what I experienced before.

"So, you should be prepared for Fly to have periods of regression for the rest of his life, but I don't expect it to be as bad as it has been. Also, now you know how you can work with him. Next time, he will be much faster at reacting the right way. One of the most important things is to take a step back to where he said 'yes' again, and then try it again. Perhaps with a smaller step, a smaller task," she explained.

"I am so glad we called you, Sofia. We could never have handled this ourselves. Thank you so very, very much for your help, you're really talented," said Alice, who was sitting next to Sofia. She put her arm around Sofia's shoulder, giving her a big hug.

Sofia packed up her computer and they agreed she would return the next day at 9 am to conclude the training.

CHAPTER 32

Fly's New Life

On this beautiful summer morning the horses were playing their usual game of tag with Benji. Aphrodite had begun to play along. She could run almost as fast as Fly. In fact, there were times she would outrun Scamp. Scamp wasn't the fastest sprinter, but he had the endurance to run for longer than the other two. His breed gave him more stamina than speed. Fly loved to play with the little ones. Now that he had learned that he was safe and comfortable with his humans, he was more relaxed. He could play without having to be on alert all the time. This made life less stressful, like he had felt before he went to the racetrack. In fact, it was even easier than when he was a baby out with the other colts because there, he had been the responsible leader in charge.

Now, he had both Alexandra, Sir Howard, and Lisa to take care of him in the pasture. They were much older than he was, and they had much more life experience. His new humans had become part of his herd as well, thanks to learning horsemanship from Sofia. He was finally convinced that these humans wanted only good for him, and that he could talk to them. They understood him, and he them!

He had become especially fond of Nicholas. Every time he came down to the pasture Fly would whinny and come running, his mane and forelock billowing around him.

During the weeks of training according to Sofia's plan,

Nicholas had increasingly been included in the training. Turned out that Fly made even more progress when Nicholas worked with him. Nicholas' natural understanding and empathy with animals meant that animals were quick to trust him. He also had the patience to give the animals the time they needed to understand things.

Once he had learned the technique, it turned out that she had a good sense of the press and release method. He could tell from the animals when it was time to press, and when he needed to release.

"Benji!" Jacob called.

Fly needed his hooves trimmed by the farrier today. They were all a little worried about how it would go. They could easily lift his hooves and even knock on them with a brush but it wasn't the same when a stranger was going to do it. They had told the farrier about the problems Fly had in the past. The farrier had reassured them that he would proceed slowly.

"Flyyy!" Nicholas called.

Both the horses and Benji stopped in the middle of the chase and looked at Jacob and Nicholas before taking off running toward them.

Fly didn't stop until he was standing right in front of Nicholas. He tossed around his head a few times. Nicholas laughed and threw his arms around his neck, giving him a big hug.

"Hi, Fly. Today is a big day. Your hooves really need to be seen by the farrier! Don't be scared, it won't hurt!" he reassured his friend.

Fly didn't understand a word, but he loved the sound of Nicholas' voice and his hugs. He also knew that something was about to happen, because Nicholas had his halter in his hand, and he noticed that Jacob had brought Sir Howard's halter.

What are we doing today?

Fly was eager to do something with Nicholas, so he nudged

the halter to get it on, so he could get started on another fun day. Laughing, Nicholas put the halter and lead rope on Fly's head.

"Boy, you're excited, Fly! You sure have become a completely different horse!" he said with a pat to Fly's neck.

Fly looked at Nicholas with a gentle and loving expression in his big, beautiful, bright, black eyes.

"Life is great, my friend!" the eyes said … "life is great!" Jacob and Alice had seen and heard Nicholas and Fly's exchange.

"Eyes can say more than all the words in the world," Alice said, "Isn't that right, Jacob?"

"I think so," Jacob answered, "The soul behind the eyes tells the unadulterated truth. All souls can talk to each other. We just need to learn to understand what the soul says, like animals can."

"Soul language," she said thoughtfully, "that'll be the next thing for us to learn. Now that we've learned horse language, Equus. I wonder if we can't learn to speak with our souls as well," Alice said.

Nicholas had heard the last part of their conversation.

"Is that like when I get the feeling that Fly is actually talking to me … or … maybe it's more like I know what he is thinking and feeling?" he asked.

"Yes, I think that's what it is!" Alice said. "And when it seems like I can hear my grandma?" he asked.

"Yes, when you can hear your grandma too, Nico," Jacob said tenderly.

Nicholas smiled a happy smile, looked at Fly, turned around, and started to walk toward the gate. Fly was happy to follow. He didn't know yet that the farrier was waiting for him in the stable.

Jacob and Sir Howard, Alice, and Benji followed along behind. Alice let the others out the gate.

Alice and Jacob were wondering how Fly would react. Obviously, they were hoping that it would go well but if it became too difficult for him, they would rather stop and reschedule the farrier. They'd work with him some more and try again later. They were going to record it on video, which they could show to Sofia in case they needed her help.

Nicholas chit-chatted with Fly, as they always did on their way up to the stable. There was an almost visible bond between them. They practically melted together into one being in beautiful harmony. They were happy, they had everything they needed: security, love, funny animals and humans, food and drink! What more could anybody want?

"I am so happy that Alice and Jacob gave you this chance, Fly. I knew you were much too good to just be slaughtered!" Nicholas said as he petted Fly's neck. Fly nodded his head.

The farrier was standing in the door to the stable looking at them. His many years of experience with thousands of horses helped him form an impression of Fly, which he could use to develop a good relationship with him from the start.

Fly spotted him. Stopped short. Lifted his head high. Huffed loudly. Nicholas stopped too, spotting the farrier in the door to the stable.

Now, the farrier turned sideways and stood with his side facing them and a relaxed posture. Nicholas petted Fly's neck and took a deep breath.

"It's just fine, Fly. It's just the farrier. He is the nicest farrier in the world, and he is our friend," he said calmly.

Nicholas' body language and gentle words convinced Fly that there was no reason to be afraid.

The farrier is standing with his side facing us, so he is inviting us to come closer. Let's see what happens. Perhaps it's something fun? And there's always carrots and apples in the stable.

This was much more like the inquisitive, self-confident, and adventurous Fly might think; the Fly that existed before the other humans had inflicted such bad wounds on his soul. The wounds had healed now but there were scars.

Nicholas walked toward the farrier and Fly

followed. Fly would follow Nicholas anywhere and for the rest of his life.

ACKNOWLEDGEMENT

Thank you to my mom and dad for always believing in me and supporting my choices.

Thank you to Mr. Monty Roberts for teaching us to make the world a better place for horses. You are the reason of my success with horses as a trainer and rider. You inspire me daily.

Thank you to Miss Robin Pressley to open your heart and beautiful home and made it the place where *A horse named Fly* was finished in the Danish version known as *Flying High* – I love you oceans my sister from another mister – thank you for letting me ride our once-in-a-lifetime horse – Caribi, in his last and my first Grand Prix. Thank you for making my dreams come true. You inspire me with your kind personality.

Thank you to Mrs. Shaneen Noble-Antar to open your heart and wonderful farm and home and believing in me teaching lessons and clinics. Thank you for editing *A horse named Fly* with such a loving heart and for believing in the book. Thank you for being a true animal lover who listen to them with an open heart and mind. I love you infinite.

Thank you to the *Flying High team* consisting of the family Noble-Antar for being constructive criticism and good suggestions to make the story sharp.

Thank you to all the horses in my life – each one of you has a special place in my heart. I'll never forget any of you.

A HORSE NAMED FLY

a story og learning a new language

Horses do talk - just listen and learn

Printed in Great Britain
by Amazon

35486353R00090